Long Journey Home

Book One

To: Yvonne
From: Celina

— Many
Blessings

A novel by:

Celina Machen Easterling

Editor:

Betty Ann Reynolds

Long Journey Home

Book One

Long Journey Home

By

Celina Machen Easterling

Acknowledgments

If it were not for my recent lifestyle change and supportive family, this attempt would not have been successful, and without the love and support of my husband, Adam, this would not have even been possible. His encouragement for me to excel in whatever I do is most humbling and enabling. I am so grateful for God's grace and the blessing of our marriage these 22 years. To my three blessings, God so graciously blessed me with your lives. I count myself a blessed person to have the honor to be your Mom. Thank you for reading, talking, and pondering all of my stories.

I am so very thankful for the encouragement from my dear farmgirl sister, Lauren, who encouraged me to write many, many years ago when our kids were young. I am also appreciative to my dear friend, Karen, who always made sure I felt her love and encouragement for each posted article. I am lovingly thankful for my sisterly friend, Christie, for her support, encouragement, and brain power for bouncing ideas with me. She is a jewel that I treasure. Last, but not meant for least is for my mother, Nancy, I am blessed by her constant encouragement and love of proofreading – I simply adore her.

I began this story not as a mirror of my family, but as a small and simple way to honor the heritage of those who came before me. It is my earnest prayer that God would show favor and compassion in the salvation of all who I love and hold dear. ***Thank You, Betty Ann, for being so patient and kind in the process.

Giving thanks always for all things unto God and the Father in the name of our Lord Jesus Christ: (Ephesians 5:20) KJV

Prologue

August 1845

Sadie stood up straight from the wash pail, stretching the bend in her back with one hand and wiping the sweat-filled hazelnut curls from her face with the other. Her mind was busy amid the morning chores. A few more pieces, she thought, and the wash would soon be finished. There wasn't much of a breeze in this humid, late summer morning. Her thoughts meandered away again, with her brain rattling full of necessary preparations for the turning of the seasons. With both of her parents gone now, the burdens of this wild frontier rested on the shoulders of Sadie and her older brother Ollie.

Awakened from her thoughts, she heard a rustle in the thicket. Instantly tense, Sadie reached for the shotgun leaning against the woodpile. This Texas backcountry was very wild and untamed, hiding all manner of critters. It could be a cougar or a mountain lion which were known to frequent these parts, or even a rabid skunk or raccoon. Tightening her grip on her Poppa's old shotgun, she pointed in the direction of the rustle, and coming into view out of the dense yaupon was a buck. He was so majestic with his heavy head of antlers and buckskin fur. He was bigger than any buck she'd ever seen, at least at this short distance. He was struggling to get free from his vining restraints, and from the sheer panic in his eyes, he looked as though she had interrupted him. Taking pause, still pointing the barrel of the gun in his direction Sadie was unsure of how to proceed. She stared at him; he'd clearly had been having a tussle in the muscadine grape vines for a while. What on earth pushed him in there, she thought?

With a burst of vigor, he broke free of the vines and thickets. In his successful attempt to get away from the oppressive foliage, he leapt towards the cabin, right straight across from the opposing clothes line. He kept his gaze fixed on his dazed audience, not seeing his impending obstacle course before him. Ducking the clothesline in his flight, he inadvertently caught Ollie's shirt with his heavy rack. The crème-colored muslin shirt hung draped in the antlers, leaving the buck blinded and shaking his head back and forth. He maintained his course, disoriented, right into the side of the cabin, and as his bad luck continued to unfold, he managed to perfectly wedge his horn immoveable, "You would have thought those ornery antlers were brand new the way he tussled them about," Sadie thought. He stopped moving for a brief second to focus on the wall before him, staring cross-eyed he could see the ripped fabric pieces dangling over his head, staring even further down the tip of his nose, his focus neared the log wall, as he stood awkwardly braced with erratic panting.

Sadie set the shotgun back down against the wood pile and took a step forward, but she quickly froze mid stride cautious and aware, not wanting to get caught by those wild antlers. The great buck was now frantically moving back and forth, wiggling to get free from the restraint of the cabin wall. Panic was setting in, she wanted to somehow help him but was not sure how, she looked around to see what she could use to aid him in his trial. "Ah, the hay fork." She could use it to pry and create leverage to break his hold. She leapt into action quickly and left for a brief moment to fetch the wooden fork from round the side of the cabin. She slowly came around the corner of the cabin looking and listening with the pitchfork gripped firmly in her hands. Her eyes met those of a startled and now completely hysterical buck.

In a desperate final attempt to get free, the buck sat back on his rear end and pulled with all he had from the clutches of the wall. In the exertion of applying all of his strength, he catapulted backward into the wash water. His rear end was submerged in the sotol basket with his front foot still in the water pail. He was a sight to be seen, sitting straddle-legged like a dog, in complete disarray, with Ollie's shirt and vines hanging in his face. He was now free, but with a broken antler and wounded pride. He managed to pull himself to his feet, and clangity, clang, clang, he stepped awkwardly forward, fumbling as his hoof made contact with the bucket and the vibrating handle. As the buck staggered around into everything in sight, the remaining clothes were now on the ground and the line was in shambles.

Resembling a staggering drunk the buck managed to step out of what was now an empty and misshapen bucket and a pile of soiled laundry. He paused and glanced back at her for a second before springing away into the tall grass that lead to the dense woods. He immediately disappeared into the wood that he came from, with Ollie's ripped shirt and pieces of the grape vines trailing behind, still entangled in his antlers. As quickly as he had appeared, so he vanished away into the pinewood.

Sighing with a deep breath of relief- Sadie thought to herself, "Oh dear, what a mess and what will Ollie say?" She should have shot him, she thought; she had more than one opportunity. He would have provided more than enough meat for the two of them for weeks. The commotion had come and gone so quickly she was paralyzed, watching in unbelief as he floundered around. Worse than losing dinner, the laundry was ruined; Ollie only had two shirts and the buck made off with most of one.

Chapter 1

September 1845

"Morning, Sadie," Ollie called out.

"You're up already?" groggily replied his sister, rubbing her sleepy eyes.

"Yep, I've got to get busy early."

"It's still dark out, the chickens aren't even up yet, brother!"

"That rooster will be up soon enough, and if he doesn't waste any daylight, then neither can I. I've got a hankering for some of your skillet cornbread, there's a fire on the hearth, and the chicory is a goin', so get up girl!" Ollie barked orders with a gentle command that she loved and a soft smile she looked for in the corner of his mouth while rustling around in the primitive cabin.

"I won't have you making a mess, Oliver Wright Hartmann," Sadie declared as she slid from beneath the cozy quilt Mama made her. Even in the summer she couldn't bear to sleep without it. In one motion, Sadie grabbed a hairpin, twisting her curls into a quick bun. She found her favorite apron on the peg by her bed where she always left it.

"Using my whole name? Huh... Is that supposed to get my attention? That only works if you are Mama."

She snickered as she draped the shawl over her shoulders. They had both known for sure they were in trouble when their Mama had used their full name.

"Well, what's so important today, brother, that not even the chickens can sleep?" Sadie demanded as she slipped into her boots and made her way to the table.

"Yesterday, tracking in the woods, I came across what looked like cow tracks. Might be some around here close," Ollie started explaining while pouring each of them a cup of chicory coffee.

"Cows? You didn't mention any cows yesterday!"

"It came to me last night like. You'd already drifted to sleep. Yep, I'm going to take ole Jed and we jes' going to round them up; drive them over to the field below us." Her brother kept going, with more light and determination in his eyes than she'd seen since they'd been there. He knew nothing of working cattle other than a few stories their Poppa shared from his younger days.

"Mmhmm..," acknowledged Sadie as she listened while she mixed ingredients together. "Grab that dutch oven for me, would you?" He hopped up, grabbing a towel to protect his hand from the hot handle on the pot. Sadie began pouring the cornbread into the shallow hot grease. Ollie never missed a beat as he paced the length of the cabin.

"I have plans, you see. We are going make this place work, just like Poppa dreamed."

"Well, you know ole Jed has a mind of his own some days. He's starting to feel his age – that trip here wore hard on him after Poppa had to put down Ned. For a riding mule he can work all day- if'n he wants to" chimed Sadie. - "but if he doesn't; he'd rather stand there and look at you like you're missing your pants."

"Oh, that mule will do as I say", Ollie reassured her.

"Do you need some help? I would love to go out with you today and track some cows."

"No, these cows aren't like Maude, that you can sweet talk with a handful of corn. Naw, I reckon, I need to do this on my own," Ollie said gently as he wiped his mouth with the napkin. He loved his sister and couldn't bear anything happening to her. Longhorns were unpredictable and he needed to prove himself by some unwritten standard he measured in his head against the memory of his Poppa.

The two bantered back and forth until they saw the first hint of orange glowing behind the pines, heralding their favorite part of the day. Standing quickly, Ollie dusted the crumbs off of his shirt, grabbed his gear, and headed towards the door.

"I should be back by dinner. Love you, Sis," he said as he closed the cabin door.

"Another quiet day to me, myself, and I," Sadie thought aloud, dreading the loneliness. "I will surely get out to work in the garden and then go look for some pecans."

Ollie popped his head back in the door, "Oh Sadie, I forgot my cornbread and my bandana. Oh, and mind that you stay close to the cabin, would you!"

"But…."

"NO Butts about it… Sarah Margaret Hartmann, I promise I'll go exploring with you tomorrow."

"That only works if you're Poppa, and just because you are two years older than me doesn't make you my boss." Sadie sassed with a teasing grin.

"That is true, I think it's a bit early in the season for pecan pickin' but I'd like to go with you tomorrow if you can manage to wait." Tipping his hat to her with a soft wink he turned and sauntered back out the door towards the corral.

She eased up from table, blowing out the candle, and sat down in her Mama's rocking chair close to the window. Pulling her knees up in the sway of the chair, she paused to pull back the curtain to see Ollie leading Jed away from the corral. Warming her hands with her cup of chicory she thought," It will be a long day for sure if he's already leading old Jed." The scope of the picture before her, of her stubborn brother and the fickle old mule made her laugh out loud.

It hadn't even been a year since March that they arrived on this wild frontier. Ollie and Poppa got supplies back in Crockett, after we stopped in at the land office to make inquiries before paying the steep price to ferry the wagon with Jed, Maude, and the hog across the Trinity, the last major river crossing. Now that the supplies were getting low and fall was around the corner, they both felt an unspoken urgency. It was Poppa's dream to settle here in Texas. He had shared on more than one occasion that this is our chance- to have something- land and heritage for our kids to inherit.

Some days she really worried about Ollie. He pushes himself so hard to do just what Poppa would have, Sadie thought. Oh, how she missed her parents and the security they provided. She wished Mama was here. Their Mama's sickness got worse on the long trip, when she took a fever and never got better. Truth is, she reflected, Mama had she'd been sick for a while; but Mama and Poppa didn't want us kids to worry. She appeared so strong; she didn't want us to stop or delay on her behalf. We excused Mama's melancholy nature on the account of the sickness. Poppa had made her a bed in the wagon, getting rid of anything that she would part with and some things that she wouldn't. She passed and went to be with Jesus before we got to our new home. Mama never saw our homestead, and Poppa was never the same. It was like we lost a part of him that day. It's hard to believe how far we'd come in such a short time. It must have been painful hard for him to leave her in Mississippi and we continue on. We picked a spot on a hill overlooking the great Mississippi River so her memory could face the way we went. Sadie heard Maude bellow, causing her to break her gaze through the window, she wiped the tear from her face with her apron tail, her cup sat empty in her lap, her chicory was all gone. Her morning break is over, it's time to get stirring about the day.

"God, please protect Ollie and bring him home safe," she whispered soft.

Chapter 2

"Come on now, you sorry excuse for a mule!" Ollie kicked Jed hard in the flank with the worn-out heels of his boots. Jed was getting old and he had just one speed, slow. "Those cows will be halfway to San Antonio if you don't – GET UP!"

It was humid and sticky, and Ollie was getting shorter on patience by the second. Thinking of his canteen and cornbread, packed snug in the saddle bags for lunch, Jed halted at the creek. Ollie dismounted and stretched his tense legs, hearing them crackle. Standing straight, the young man was a lanky, scrawny string bean towering 6'2" and with his mother's fair skin, blue eyes, and dandelion hair. He pulled his hat off to wipe his brow while looking in the vast woods surrounding him. Loosening his rein on Jed so the mule could get a cool drink. He pulled out a hunk of cornbread and broke off a piece for himself and the mule. Opening his gloved hand flat he let Jed nibble the crumbs with his worn out teeth as he looked around, gaining his bearings.

He most definitely inherited that dreamer streak from his Poppa. The only thing he knew to do was to just keep busy to follow that dream. They'd come too far now- there was nothing nor anyone back east. Poppa had sold all they had to buy this parcel of land and the rest was spent on the journey. Now, it was up to Oliver and his kid sister to do something with it. Loosening the girth on old Jed, Ollie scratched his belly promising, "If you'd do this one thing-- I'll retire you to the corral for carrots and corn treats, when Sadie isn't looking, of course."

Poppa had bought Ned & Jed, their team of wagon mules for the trip. Mama said they'd never make the journey, and that they certainly were not worth the price Poppa paid for them. Mama was superb at making one penny go the distance of two. As was his way, Poppa handled all the arrangements for the journey. Boston was dirty and overcrowded. Texas was the plan, the dream, and the hope for a new beginning. Poppa said, "You can't replace experience and know-how so easily. This team had more than their share of journeys and experience in the wild. God seasoned them perfect for such a journey as this."

Jed took two steps back and reared his head up in earnest, with his flopping ears laid over. Ollie grabbed the scatter gun out of the scabbard and listened intently through the hiccupping bray that was bouncing an echo off of the trees. Trying to calm Jed he talked softly, "whoa, now, easy, old man". His skin tingled with the feeling that he was not alone. The first thought was always the Injuns. These parts were known to have stragglers or stray Indians that held no loyalties to anyone and often were thieves. He and Sadie felt like it was really a matter of time before an encounter.

Watching and listening, he heard nothing but the faint stream trickling in the creek and a muffled breeze in the pines. He couldn't shake this uneasy feeling, however, he untethered the lead rope off of the saddle horn and motioned with a click for ole Jed to walk on with him, leading him across the sand creek and pulling himself and the old mule up the sandbank on the other side. Pushing their way through the thicket, the two stepped into a small, lush clearing. How had he missed this, this perfect, cleared, cubby hole of prairie?

There were 20, no- 25 head of cattle here, just grazing on grama grass.   "This is it, Jed!" He said, whispered in excitement to his mule. "We need to push them real gentle like cross the creek and up on home to the farm. I've heard these here longhorns can be a bit ornery; so you do as I say, Jed.   I can't wait to see the look on Sadie's face when we come home with a herd of cattle."

With no time to waste, he threw his lanky leg over to mount Jed. At the same moment, he and Jed heard a branch snap and movement in the trees. Ollie scanned the area, looking for the hidden watcher that he could feel present. Jed, still on edge, reared again in panic while protesting with his obnoxious bray; the cows bolted, and ran straight away. Throwing their heads up in disapproval they kicked up their heels, turning up the dry soil. The mob was headed away from Ollie, but the echoing of the hooves in unison sent shivers up his spine. Things had escalated quickly he'd lost his chance to bring home the cattle and would be forced to try again another day.

"Well done, Jed!" Ollie sassed as he slumped in the saddle.

Without warning, the herd shifted their path; they began to swing round following the tree line. The angry mob was blaring and gaining speed, and Ollie's jaw dropped open, as he stared in disbelief. He wanted them to come his way, but this wasn't quite the plan he had in mind. He hadn't the experience to round up stampeding cows.

"What in tarnation are they doing?" He thought for a split second more as his brain tried to register the view before him. "Is that someone riding among them?" The herd of testy longhorns had made a big horseshoe and were now gaining momentum headed towards Ollie. There was no time to run, but Ollie tugged and yelled at the old mule, pleading for his compliance.

"JED- GIT UP! Git UP, Git UP! , he yelled as he kicked and swatted Jed's rump with the rope frantically urging him back towards the creek. He'd remembered seeing a large oak tree over in the bend of the creek bottom. Now barreling down after Ollie and the old mule, the longhorns came in like a swarm of bees, chasing right after them. If he could just get behind the large oak tree in the creek bed, he and Jed could survive the stampede. Jed, sensing Ollie's urgency and seeing that herd of longhorns plowing rows at him, they sparked into a quick trot that changed awkwardly into an erratic scurry. The mule ran throwing his front feet out, his tail sucked tight to his rear, and his enormous ears at attention pointing forward in the direction he wished to go. He shuffled with a stamina that led Ollie to believe that they might just make it.

"Dear God, Help us…" he shouted as they made their descent into the creek bottom.

Chapter 3

Ham stretched out his bedroll and leaned back on an old dead hickory tree. The Texas night was clear and bright with a full moon hung high in the sky. He'd rode in that saddle for more days than he could count and was glad to be relieved of it, even if for just a few hours. He didn't know where he belonged in this grand territory. He'd fought the brown man, the red man, and a few white men, fighting was just second nature. He'd been given some time off from the Ranger Company "to relax and cool down." What did that mean anyway, he thought? One thing he knew for sure – he didn't want to be anywhere without his line back dun, Flip, and his Colt revolver. With those trusted comrades he pretty much figured he could handle anything that came his way.

Ham had raised his stud horse from a colt. His Gramps had charged him with the responsibility to wean, raise, and care for the colt. The colt was smart as a whip and would do just anything for Ham. Up to now he and Flip had been in many skirmishes, and they always took care of each other. He and his faithful horse had been all the way to the east coast to see the Atlantic Ocean and to "relax" as Captain Hayes had ordered. He'd found one thing that he liked on this journey, and that was his quiet life. The quiet had always been so hollow and lonesome. He'd learned to embrace it and to trust the simplistic life he knew. He wasn't into loose women, gambling, or drinking. He'd tried his hand at all of that and found it less than satisfying. Still, he ached with a restlessness he couldn't pinpoint or a need with a pressed desire that he had no clue of.

He'd been raised by his widowed gran who'd taught him the ways of Jesus. She'd long since departed this world and Ham had been all on his own- seeing first hand there wasn't much Jesus in the world. It took little convincing but he signed up with the Texas Rangers in his late teens and had been fighting battles ever since. He had regrets- he just wanted to put them in the past. The miles he'd covered didn't seem to separate him from the agony he wished to forget and escape. He'd relaxed about all he could. It was time to get back to law and order down on the border; at least that's what he kept telling himself.

He'd come through a little frontier town called Crockett, a few miles back before making camp off of the Trinity River. He'd resupplied his saddle bags with chicory and beef jerky, and got new horse shoes on Flip. No family left, no home, certainly no woman, he'd given it all up for rangerin'.

He'd heard back in town that there were some settlers out this way except, no one had seen or heard from them since the spring. He'd nose around and see if he could discover their demise and make a report at Fort Boggy of his findings. He'd steered clear of the old San Antonio Road, known for riff-raff and needy travelers. He tossed a piece of dead wood onto the fire; the mosquitos were getting mighty thick. He'd had a bath and shave back in town and it felt right good at the time – now he felt like bait for them skeeters. Ham removed his hat, unbuckled his gun belt and shed his boots to unwind for his rendezvous with the sundown. There was nothing more relaxing than the sound of the river rushing in a hurry, headed south to nowhere and with the frogs and crickets singing in unison.

At first light, he'd saddle Flip and wade across in the shallow bend of the river; he wasn't much for getting his tack wet if he could help it, and rightly so. Once across, Ham figured he'd make his way back south off of the beaten path for new orders. Flip grazed close to camp, swishing his tail at flies and snorting at every other stem of grass. Coyotes howled in the distance, singing their night song. His eyes were heavy; with his hand on his Colt, he shifted on the crunchy patch of grass and drifted off.

Chapter 4

Pouring the leftover chicory coffee onto the fire, Ham gathered up his supplies. Flip was looking rested and well grazed after a good night's rest. Ham untied the hobbles on Flip, taking notice the Dunn seemed a bit frisky in his step this morning.

"All right, Hold it… we're a-going!" Tightening the girth, he led Flip in a wide circle. As he walked him about, Ham was forcing the horses' breath heavily because Flip was known to hold his breath. The clever stud horse, standing at eighteen and a half hands high, would wait until he was saddled and bridled then let an unsuspecting rider into the seat. Flip would then give a mighty exhale, and with a big shake of the withers, the saddle would be so loose that whoever was perched there would fall off. Ham reached down and pulled up on the billet strap to tighten two holes, then eased into the saddle. He gave a gentle nudge and Flip took out in a swift walk.

As they approached the river, Ham spied a sand bar and determined it would be a good place as any to cross. It hadn't rained for some weeks and the river was down considerably, so there was no problem with the crossing. Continuing to track west, Flip stepped briskly along at a steady pace through the dry bottom lands. Despite the gnats and mosquitos, he loved Texas even in summer.

Ham had a reputation of being sharp around edges an impression he liked to maintain. On the inside he was really soft at heart, yearning for a different life. He caught himself thinking he wouldn't mind settling down here- somewhere. Quickly correcting, he thought, not in the bottom lands but among these tall pines that reached the sky, where the trees were green year round, and open fields lay covered with waist-high grass with plentiful game.

Wait, what was he thinking? His life was on the trail. No woman would want him after what he had done and the wounds he had suffered. His arm twitched with a spasm of pain, and he massaged the upper muscle to quiet his regrets. There was no life in one place for him. That was not the way of a Ranger. He'd done everything to be just that- a Texas Ranger.

Before he'd realized it, they were climbing up a slow incline out of the bottom lands and into a dense track of trees and thickets. He found a trail and nudged Flip on. Weaving in and around the tall pines, he made good time tracking over creeks, meadows, and gullies. Ham halted Flip as he saw a flock of birds explode from a group of trees. Taking two steps forward, Flip nervously stopped again and flicked his ears. Ham was listening intently too. It sounded like he heard someone yelling. There could be settlers, Mexicans, or Indians- or any combination of the three. He couldn't quite make out what all the fuss about, but he was never one to back down, so he gave his horse a nudge with his silver-dollar spurs. Ham was proud of those one of a kind spurs. His Gramps had his spurs made especially for Ham, replacing the rowels with new silver dollars. They were the last gift his Gramps gave him, and one of the few possessions he still had.

Easing Flip on toward the commotion, he found himself in a clearing with a herd of charging longhorns. He'd walked head first right into a longhorn stampede! "This is about to get hairy," he thought aloud. Ham reacted quickly, with a double nudge of his right spur and a slight pull to the left on the reins. Ham squeezed gently with his knees as Flip responded with a swift swerve by taking back to the left, cutting in behind the tree line rounding the corners of the prairie. Ham kicked Flip into a quick lope beyond the trees.

Out of the view of the herd he tried to gain some distance to get round behind them. A quick tap of the spurs and a hard right, launched Flip out of the trees and into the middle of the herd of cattle. This was no Sunday picnic; Ham stood in the stirrups and leaned forward; now in a high lope. He gave Flip his head and they continued to gain speed, keeping free of horns he focused his attention on the lead bull. If they were lucky, he could flank the herd turning them back. He pushed his way forward to catch up with the bull and the unruly bovine lowered his head to let out a bawl of protest. The ranger pulled out his pistol and shot off a round in the air challenging the leader. Kicking up his south end in revolt, the bull turned the mob of longhorns away. Ham pulled back on the reins to ease up Flip, letting the herd take its leave.

Flip, now prancing in place, was keyed up and ready for round two. The cows followed the tree line and were headed around the opposite way. They turned up the golden clearing and looked as though they were headed for the creek bottom at the base of the trees. Ham followed behind them at a slow lope, with his pistol already drawn. He wasn't sure where this person or persons could've gone but he had a bad feeling. The cattle crossed down into the sandy bottom creek and up the other side, then scattered into the woods, making tracks in all directions. Ham eased Flip down the bank, listening for any voices. He had no idea if he'd just run up on to some rustlers. Picking his way down into the creek bottom, he caught a glimpse of something behind a tree; he wasn't sure what he was seeing, but it looked like an animal was down.

Dismounting, he called out, "Hello- you alright? I don't mean any harm- I'd like to help you if I can." He slowly came around the bend in the creek bottom to get a better view. There beneath the oak tree in the faint stream of water lay a badly injured grey mule and a boy. The boy was moaning something, it sounded like "Lady," but Ham couldn't interpret his mumbles. He holstered his pistol and dropped the reins on the ground and rushed to the boy.

He gently eased the boy out from under the mule and pulled a handkerchief from his own belt to wipe the boy's face. He lifted his head and tried to give him a drink from the canteen lying on the ground, but the boy was out cold with no obvious injury. He looked over at the mule- he was done. "I'm not sure but I think this here critter sacrificed himself for this kid," he said aloud. The old mule was struggling to breathe and in clear discomfort. He had been trampled and wasn't going to recover. Ham knew the only humane thing to do was to give the animal peace. Ham moved gingerly to remove the boy and prop his head up with the saddle from the mule. He slid out his pistol and shot the mule, and the boy came up swinging with wide-open bloodshot eyes, threatening to tear him apart. Just as Ham tried to reason with the boy the youngster passed out again and fell limp on Ham. "That bump on his head probably just saved me. If that boy had his wits about him he might just have succeeded in his quest," he jested, as he picked him up and went for higher ground to make camp.

Chapter 5

Ollie was struggling to open his eyes. He listened and heard the faint sound of the stream, the crackling of a fire and the smell of coffee. His eyes seemed so heavy and his body smarted something awful. His headached, with a dull ringing in his ears. As he raised his arm to touch his forehead a voice unknown to him called out, "Easy there, cowboy, you took a pretty bad beating, if'n you still wanna fight- we'll fight, let's wait till you get your strength back".

"Where is Jed?" Ollie mumbled.

"Sorry, son, you are the only person I found down there. What the heck do you think you were doing chasing those wild doggies?" Ham leaned back on a gum tree across from the small camp fire that crackled between them.

"No, - where's- my -mule?" Ollie slowly asked.

"I'm sorry, friend; your mule was in bad shape. Have another sup of water; I've got some chicory to clear your throat and a bite of jerky if you gotta hunger pain." Ham held out a warped tin cup and a piece of jerky to the boy.

Ollie slowly sat up, resting his weight on his elbow, taking the water and refusing the jerky. He was trying to take in his surroundings. His eyes were having trouble with focusing and he needed to get a good look at this cowpoke that had done messed up his day. Wetting his lips with the water, he realized how dry he was. "How long was I out?" Ollie muttered.

"A day and night, friend- I drug your old mule out of the creek bottom and built camp up here. I've been waiting fer ya to wake up. Who's the lady, your girl? She'll be worried, I spect." Ham tore a piece of jerky with his teeth.

Ollie felt fear wash over him- "Sadie! I have to get home, now!"

"Let me and Flip help you get home. It's the least I can do." Ham offered.

"No, I think you've done enough, don't you?" Ollie spat out. Ham sat silently watched and him try to pull himself up by tugging on a defenseless sapling of a tree. He decided to let the boy alone, as long as he kept away from the fire. It was plain that he wanted his empty rifle scabbard that Ham had deliberately set far away.

"You caused the stampede, lost me my cows, shot my mule; did I leave anything out?" Ollie fumed, his pale face turning red with heat and frustration.

"Well now, wait just one minute, son." Ham sat up from his tree, resting his muscular arm across his knee with a stark look in eyes. "There's no need to get all itchy in the saddle."

"I'm not your son; you can take your horse and just keep right on a going whichever way it was you came from. I don't need or want your help, Mister." Ollie began mumbling further and looking dazed and more confused. He released the sapling and staggered all over the small campsite, turning, pale, and then dropping to the ground again with another unconscious thud.

Ham picked up the kid and flung him up on Flip. "All right, boy, we have to get this kid home, before he dies and some angry widow woman comes a huntin' me down." He gathered up the boy's saddle bags and canteen, doused the fire and led his horse through the thickets. After going only a few feet he spotted what looked like a worn-out trail with recent mule tracks; as he follows the trail, it led to another creek. As it was nearing dusk he gingerly guided Flip in step as he walked the horse down the embankment and up the other side, which was steep and slippery from the artesian aquifers seeping from the ground. He noticed that this area had been recently logged. Continuing to follow the tracks he reached the apex and stepped into a clearing containing a log cabin, small corral, a veggie garden, out house, and firewood stacked. He hoped this was the right place, as it was now late and Ollie was beginning to moan again. He thought of knocking him out just to keep him from putting up another fight. Ham paused to make sure Ollie wasn't going to fall off of the saddle before approaching the house when a lady appeared from what looked like a little animal hutch.

What would he say to his wife? How would he explain what happened? He wasn't sure what happened exactly, he felt partly responsible, and hadn't prepared himself for her possible anger or even rage. He'd do what he can and then move on at first light. He could send for a doctor once he reached Fort Boggy. That was the best he could offer.

●

Sadie stood up straight out of the coop and turned to swivel the wooden latch in place. Her awareness was diverted across the clearing towards the far trail. The familiar sound of a horse nicker in the distance grabbed her curiosity, she cupped her hand over her eyes to dim the glare so she could see more clearly in the dusky evening haze. She caught a glance on the tree line of a man with a horse, but she didn't recognize the dark silhouette that seemed to lean heavy towards his left side. She squinted and took a few steps further into the shade of a pine tree. It looked like her Ollie draped across the saddle lifeless and limp. She could see his white hair and salmon suspenders; realizing in an instant her worst fears had just become her reality, she dropped the eggs into her apron pocket and ran toward the stranger.

"Good gravy!" Catching her breath, "What happened and just who are you?" Sadie gently picked up Ollie's head as her tears begin forming. She examined his pasty skin and the dried blood on his forehead. Putting her hand over her mouth, falling to her knees she looked up and made eye contact with the stranger, "He's not --.... Is he?"

Diverting his eyes away he responded, "No, Ma'am- bump to the head is all, with some scrapes and bruises. He had a run in with some cows, and I found him in a creek not far from here."

"May the Lord bless you for bringing him home. Come, help me get him in the house, would ya? Do you have a name, Mister?" Sadie rattled as she tugged on the reins of the horse to speed up the process. "How did you come upon him? What was he doing?"

For once, Ham had a complete collapse of words. He wasn't sure where to start or even how to relay what little he knew. He was having trouble leading the horse and talking at the same time. He wasn't sure what came over him, he was feeling strange and sickly himself with no apparent explanation. It must have been some bad jerky or the water he thought. He lowered his head, closed his eyes, and rubbed his stomach with his free hand while concentrating to answer.

"Ah, Ma'am, yes, Hhm. well"... Ham stuttered.

"Did you hit your head too, Mister?" Sadie said, real slowly with a pause in her step and a hand on her hip followed, with a direct pointed look.

"No, NO, ma'am," Ham cleared his thought recovering from his stutter. He found her sparkling green eyes and long wave of eyelashes completely distracting, he realized the subtle sparkle might kindle into a flame at any moment. This was a married woman, he chastised the shame on himself.

Sadie entered the cabin and peeled back the wall strung quilt divider. Short of breath and anxious she spoke, "Here, lay him here- Where did you find him? When did this happen? What happened? Oh, dear Ollie- what are we gonna do?" Sadie wanted answers to it all. As she knelt next to him she paused in her thoughts, feeling a welling up of emotion with her complete inadequateness for the situation. She rose slowly, pursed her lips and took a deep breath, asking the Lord for strength, without looking to make eye contact with the stranger she began, "If you don't mind, Mister, fetch the bent pail out by the wood pile and get some water from the creek- also bring in a few sticks of firewood."

"Yes Ma'am, Sure thing, Ma'am"- Ham was relieved to be doing something outside. The fresh air would no doubt help his sudden bout of nausea.

Sadie poured the pitcher of water into a bowl and sponged the crusty blood and the dried sand off of her brother's head to get a closer look. His clothes were a mess and he had some bruises on his arms. She worked gently and carefully to clean his wounds and removed the dirty clothes. It looked as though he'd been in a fight. Come to think of it- she hadn't seen Jed. Who did this to him, and where did the stranger come from? Did he beat up Ollie and bring him home? She closed her eyes and prayed silently to God to save her brother.

"Sadie", Ollie scratched out barely in a rasp, -

"I'm right here," – she grabbed his hand and caressed his forehead. I thought I'd lost you."

"Not a chance – sister."

"Thank you dear Lord – and thank you for this man who brought my brother home." She prayed softly.

Chapter 6

The night was long; Sadie scarcely left Ollie's side. He was in and out of consciousness not making any sense. She managed to get him washed off with a cloth and minded the cut on his head. His forehead was protruding on one side and now beginning to color purple and blue. She didn't think he had any broken bones but it was hard to tell in his condition. She sat in the rocking chair beside the bed, dozing during the night and waking for every noise or movement he made. The sun was just peeking through the pines when she heard a soft tap at the door. "Ma'am?"

"Yes, come in, – I have coffee on," Sadie said quietly.

Ham entered the cabin. There were two beds against the back wall with a quilted blanket strung between to add privacy. To the left of the room was the hearth, a makeshift shelf hung on the wall, and a modest table with four chairs. To the right was a window with a matching set of rocking chairs which looked as though they had come from back east.

"Here is some more wood ma'am for the fire." He walked over toward the fireplace and set the stack of wood down. Turning and making connection with her eyes, "Did you sleep ma'am? Your candle flickered in the window till dawn."

Was this the same stranger that brought Ollie in last night? She didn't recall him having such thick brown hair peeking out under his worn hat. There was something about those deep brown eyes, which seemed hollow and intriguing. Who was this man? How did he find his way here? Where was he going? Feeling instantly self-conscious, she turned to divert her eyes, her skirts swishing about the room as she rustled around in the cabin to pour him up a cup of chicory.

"Sorry, Ma'am, for being forward; my name is Ham. I'm a Texas Ranger on my way back to Austin. I found your husband in a creek a few miles from here. He got caught up in a stampede of angry longhorns. Your mule was beyond saving. I'm real sorry. If I can help ya'll, Mrs. - I don't mind staying on a day or two."

She reached out with a shaking hand to give him his cup, and with a reddened and tear-stained face she looked up and met his glance, "No I didn't sleep much, and my brother you mean?" Sadie answered.

Ham stared awkwardly at the dirt floor for a moment, rearranging its particles with the worn toe of his boot shifting it this way and that. "Miss – that's your

37

brother there?" Ham asked as he was walking over toward Ollie's bed.

"Yes, He's my older brother and my only family left."

"Where are your parents?" he asked in a concerned tone.

"They are both passed and I am so afraid for him. If something happens to him- I will be all alone. Forgive me, I shouldn't be going on this way, especially to a complete stranger." She paused and turned to walk away.

Ollie lay perfectly still, all cleaned up. He looked much younger now- the stark realization overcame him; he is just a boy! Not knowing what to say, Ham began, "How is he, and is there anything you need?"

The young lady was wiping her face with a handkerchief; as she cleared her throat she began, "He'll be ok, I expect, if'n he wakes up – I did a lot of prayin' last night, just talkin' it over with the Lord. I can't lose Ollie, just now."- Sadie wiped her eyes with her apron tail. "First Mama, Poppa, and now Ollie – what will I do if I'm left here alone?" Her constant welling emotions making her feel increasingly awkward again, she returned back to fluttering around the cabin, making more noise than accomplishment. "I've got to hold it together," she coached herself silently with a deep sigh, as she grabbed the cast iron kettle and put it on the hearth to heat.   The ranger knew the heartache of losing loved ones all too well, yet no words came to mind just now.

He walked over to the table and set the porcelain cup down carefully. "Thank you for the coffee Ma'am."

"Thank You for all your help, Mr. Ham. We shouldn't hold you here any longer than necessary. If you could be so kind as to send the doc this way once you reach Fort Boggy. I would be most obliged. Sadie said, as though she had rehearsed with obedience.

Ham turned and walked towards the door, "Miss, I noticed that your chicken coop needs some attention. These varmints round here will steal your chickens and they'll be gone- with not so much as a feather left. I'll see what I can rustle up to make sure that those hens hang around for a while. If that's alright with you, ma'am?"

"Well, that would be very kind of you, but you really don't have to." She said, with a noticeable exhale of relief. "I'm most grateful for your help".

"It's the least I could do, Ma'am." He tipped his hat and strolled out the door.

"Oh, Mister, You need to know that we have a rooster and two hens. That rooster, he can be a real booger," she declared. Sadie found herself attracted to this man, as she gazed into those brown eyes, she wondered, what secrets and mysteries do they hold?

"I can handle a few birds, Ma'am." Ham turned away and let himself out the door.

He had to duck when clearing the threshold. "He's a chunk of a man in comparison to her Ollie; I'd better make extra cornbread, she thought. There was something appealing about that badge attached to the buckskins he wore, and the jingle of his spurs intrigued her. She walked over to the window and couldn't help watching him as he gathered materials. His walk was purposeful and his mannerisms deliberate. He reminded her of Poppa in a more handsome rough-around-the edges kind of way. As she gazed out the window and watched him work, she wondered about his family and attachments. Her Mama would have scolded her for being so forward, even in her thoughts. The whistling kettle she'd put on earlier grabbed her away from the window.

"Bless this man, Lord, who has come to help us." *She said smiling quietly to herself.*

Chapter 7

Ham milled around the clearing and found some rough-cut pine, probably left over from the building of the cabin. Over behind the small smokehouse, he found a box with a few rusty nails and a hammer. He really wasn't much for working with wood, or building anything, really, but he needed to do something. He felt partly responsible for that boy being in bed. If he hadn't turned those cows round away from him, the kid would have been ok. "Somehow, I have to make this right," he thought.

The chicken house was a little log frame box with a cane pole roof, cozy-like for a rooster and his two hens. Ham ducked down low to fit in the short, narrow doorway. Inside there were two broody red hens sitting against the back in a log hewn into a trough. They were sitting with fluffed feathers, and a snarky chicken growl, looking as though they'd seen an intruder. "Good gels- what do you have for ole Hamie today?"

He stooped down even further to reach under the feather skirt of one of the hens to check for an egg. It was stifling warm in this little bird nest hovel. Feeling around in the small nest, he found an egg, and pulling it out and setting it in his shirt tail he reached under the hen sister by her side. She also had an egg to share; as he drew away with his prize, something commenced flogging his head. Ham was stooped over nearly touching the ground, his hat fell off and the varmint seized the target of his exposed head and latched on with thrashing determination. Swiveling on his heels, Ham made his way out from the poultry prison.

Ham came out of the coop clutching the eggs in his shirt tail and flagging the air with the other hand. He was struggling to stand straight as the bird attacked the back of his head. "Dagnabbit confounded critter!" Somehow he'd failed to take note of where that rooster was, but he knew where it was now- on top of his head. This feisty bird wasn't giving up without a fight. Unconsciously, Ham was looking for something- anything- to get his attacker off of his head. He picked up the first thing he found- a ladle in the water pail. "That will work," he thought as, he commenced whacking that bird until he felt the firmness of his own blow and the rooster flown to the ground, squawking with indignation. Feeling a mite dizzy, he made his way to the cabin, with not so much as a glance back at the feathered attacker.

Stumbling into the door with a quick rap, he let himself in. "Uh, Ma'am, I need your assistance. I gathered your eggs but I had a bit of trouble. That blasted rooster had a thing or two to say about it."

"Come sit here let me have a look and by the way, I don't believe we have been introduced. My name is Sadie." She smiled with her eyes managing to deepen her straight face. "And that there rooster is Captain Crockett; he can be a little territorial." She fetched the pitcher of water and a clean cloth to the table.

"As in Davy?" Ham asked, still holding the eggs while she leaned over examining the blood from his head.

"Yes, in fact, you met Captain Davy Crockett and Mabel & Ethel, the hen sisters. Sadie couldn't help smirking a bit as she went on. "Let me take those eggs and clean up your head." She gently laid the eggs on the table in a small woven basket, then began to look through his brown curls.

"Poppa named him Davy Crockett, on the account of him being so ornery. He'd said that rooster would be the only king on this here frontier." Sadie paused, "Oh dear, he got you good, didn't he?" she snickered, relieving the awkward tension that had been between them. She took witch hazel and gently dabbed his head to clean the spur wounds.   They had a good laugh as he sat still retelling the story of his encounter with the fearsome flying foe. For just a moment, the two chattered on, feeling removed from the troubles in their own lives.

"Well I do believe- you'll live, Mr. Ham, Is that your given name? And how about some cornbread with a bit of honey for your chicken troubles?" Sadie used her apron to pull the warm lid off of the dutch oven, revealing some fresh corn bread as he replied, "That sure sounds tasty, and it's right kind of you. My given name is Hamlet Abner; I didn't much care for the Hamlet bit- that was my Ma's doin'. She was a teacher back east, and she liked the stories penned by a man named Shakespeare. Its right silly to name me after someone she'd never met. My Ma was a special lady; she died from pneumonia when I was just a little tike."

"My mother passed also on our journey here. She was sick for a long time."

"I'm so sorry for your loss." He said, glancing away from Sadie's intent gaze.

"Thank You, Mr. Hamlet."

"If you could just call me "Ham" I'd be much obliged." Wanting to change the subject away from his past, he searched for a new topic. "Are you lookin' forward to the cool spell?"

"Well yes, autumn is my most favorite time of the year. The leaves change in such beautiful colors and I'm looking forward to the air getting cooler from this baking heat." Sadie talked of the weather, her garden, and her goals for exploring and how she'd have to wait for Ollie to get better. They were enjoying a light-hearted conversation, laughing again about the feisty rooster, when Sadie then turned the conversation to a more serious tone. "Do you believe in God, Mr. Ham?"

Ham wasn't prepared for such a direct question about something so personal. His eyes were widened and he felt suddenly defensive. "If you're asking, if I believe if He exists- well, I sure do! If you're asking if He gives two bits 'bout me- I'd have to say – nope. He and I get along about like me and that there rooster of yours."

"Well, the cornbread is getting cold, so I'll go on ahead and pray," Sadie said.

"Pray?" Ham looked at her, confused.

"Yes, pray. I will bless the food." Sadie replied.
"Oh." He silently said, while feeling an odd blush come over his face, he'd just realized the purpose of her question. She reached out without asking and grabbed his hand to offer the blessing. His hand was large and rough in comparison to the daintiness of hers. To try to keep from being awkward, she began,

> *"Dear Heavenly Father, we thank you for this food and pray that you bless it to our bodies. We thank you for lookin' after Ollie and returning him home safe. Thank You for Mr. Ham, and his help to us with bringin' Ollie home and we ask that you heal him. Thank You Lord for all our blessings and the mendin' on the chicken coop (–as she tried to hold in a*

muffled snicker-) Forgive us
our sins, --In Jesus Name,
Amen."

Sadie instinctively pulled her hand away quickly and began to dish up the food onto his plate. However, she could not forget the warmth of his hand, the sun tanned skin, or the firmness of his touch. The two sat quietly, eating their lunch. Breaking the awkward silence, Ham began, "This is mighty tasty, Miss Sadie, and your brother is quite lucky to have such an able cook for a sister."

"Well, thank you, kindly. We don't have much variety out this way. My Mama taught me all she knew and I do enjoy cooking."

Ham didn't know this petite young woman, but he liked the smile lines in her cheeks already. She was so fair and the chestnut curls that escaped her bun and curled around her face were quite becoming. Her green eyes were most enchanting. He must be careful and not be so obvious in his gaze. He was lost just listening to her talk a wild tale of the buck that got away.

"Well Mr. Abner, I think we've done all the damage we can do today." Sadie stood to clear away the dishes.

"Mr. Abner would be my Pa. Please just call me Ham, plain ole Ham, Ma'am, that'd be right perfect. Thank you for the hot meal. If you'll excuse me, I'm going to go finish up that chicken shack and chop some wood- your pile is looking a mite low."

"Thank You, Mr. Abner- I mean Ham, that's kind of you. I know Ollie will appreciate all your help." Sadie fell in behind him as he made his way to the door. They both stepped out the doorway of the cabin looked about the property. "The wash bowl is round the side of the cabin under the lean-to; you are welcome to bed down around there. Supper will be at dusk -see that you wash up!" Sadie smiled from the corner of her mouth, making those laugh lines prominent as she spun on her heels, and went back inside.

"Sadie?" Ollie slurred.

"I'm here- I'm right here. Thank You, Lord! It's so good to have you back!" She scurried to his side and helped him prop up.

"We have so much to catch up on! Ham is fixing the chicken coop and is going to chop some wood."

"Ham? That cattle thieving cowpoke?"

"Yes, that Texas Ranger that brought you home to me."

"You callin' him by his first name already? What happened to the chicken coop how did he wreck that?" Ollie asked as the color began to come back to his face.

"One thing at a time. Right now, let's get some food in you. I have just made some cornbread." Sadie made a plate with cornbread, butter, and some honey. "You've got to get your strength back."

"Yeah, I do- so I can run that no account cattle wrangling cowboy out'a here." Ollie grumbled.

She grabbed Ollie's hand and bowed her head,

"Bless this food Lord, May it nourish Ollie's body and thank you, for our new friend." Sadie whispered loud enough for her brother to hear.

Chapter 8

He'd made his way by being sneaky. It was his undeniable gift being light on his feet, and as swift as a fox, he made his way from the shoals following the great river to the man's village of Robbins Ferry. The village was on the east side of the Trinity River. Alabama Ferry was closer to his home, but he couldn't go back there; he'd not been back since the fire. The fire wasn't his fault but they wouldn't believe him; no one would ever believe him.

Robbin's Ferry is an upcoming bustling port on the river, and offering a superior opportunity for his slyness. There were more buildings lining the street, with more alleys and places to hide from view. All sorts of people funneled through this river port town, some with a look he had never seen before. The busy trail to Mexico passed this way, the road is frequented by travelers and tradesman.

What treasures could he find today to add to his collection? Manatoa could not resist anything shiny. He loved the thrill of being so close to someone that he could slither by never to be seen. He didn't need any of the things he "liberated;" he only loved the rush of the snatch. He was drawn to the man villages by destiny or complete foolhardiness, of the lures he never knew which suited him more.

A loaf of bread cooling in a window would be his supper later. He crept quietly behind the buildings, looking for anything else he might fancy, anything of value, they usually kept close to themselves. The wind blew strong from the river south and a whiff of the washing cauldron over took his nostrils. "The bath house is a perfect spot he thought; they just leave their clothes right on the floor unattended." Manatoa had to go past the laundry lines and the water women. They were as he predicted, the boiling cauldrons of water, clothes flapping in the wind, and the stench of man's village, which did not appeal to Manatoa. He wove his way through the laundry undetected, and crept into the log bath house through the open side door. The double bay doors facing the river were open wide, allowing a fresh breeze. A big red faced bearded man was in the tub with a smoldering cigar, looking as though he was asleep. Tiptoeing in softly, so as to not cause a floor board to creek he found the man's trousers. He stuck his little hands into the pockets looking for anything of value, and found a shiny watch with a chain, some coins, and a picture. The woman in the picture was odd-looking, with a pointy nose and large forehead. Into his pocket immediately the watch and coins went. Picking up the man's shirt- he found two cigars. He put one of them up to his nose and ran it across his nostril to appreciate the scent; with a deep breath he took a few seconds to really absorb that aroma. The cigar spoke to him. "Smoke Me!" Manatoa laughed silently with delight.

Glancing inside the man's boot he spied a dagger. It was small and compact, with a white handle hewn solidly from wood and an edged blade inset perfectly. The handle fit nicely into his small hand, just as if it were made for him. He made a few stabs at the air, and remarked silently at its ease and the feeling in his palm. He would keep that too. Standing slowly, he tiptoed his way past the man in the tub and out the bay doors. Manatoa concentrated on staying invisible he crouched in the cat tails along the river bank, to slink away from the town undetected. Once clear of the village, he ran briskly alongside the river, taking care that he wasn't seen. Proudly, he made his way back to his empty village.

The small Indian returned to his wigwam, bearing the plunder for the day. Kicking back and relaxing against the familiar oak covered in Spanish moss, he tore a piece of the bread off and popped it into his mouth. Manatoa thought the "outsiders" were so clumsy and naturally dumb, so he felt obligated to relieve them of their burdens. It was only fair. After all, it was their fault his people left. If they had not come to his land his people would not have been forced to go. It had been too many moons to count since he'd seen his tribe. Thinking back, he remembered that it was the same time as the fire. The widow woman pleaded with him not to see the young teacher anymore. The old woman had urged him not to go exploring that day that such pursuits would end in death. However, Manatoa liked his adventures. He had no master nor would he be ruled, he often boasted to himself.

Still feeling isolated and unsettled even after his bountiful morning, Manatoa longed for some more mischief. He stretched his legs, pulling out the cigar to renew the aroma in his nasal passage again. There were settlers to plague in a day's walk in all directions of his home and he had spied on all of them. He had his favorite, he mused, smiling so widely that his eyes closed. Heaving in a deep breath, he planned just where he would go. "Tomorrow, yes, I will follow the sun and see what the pale, skinny man is up to. They need to be relieved of a chicken," he chuckled to himself, "his burden is great, and I shall release him of it."

Chapter 9

Manatoa felt the wind in his hair as he glided through the bottom lands towards the forests. He knew he was like the wind, stealthy, and swift. Heading west away from his river bottom, he went to find the lodge of the white-haired man. He knew every inch of the river bottom on both sides, he spent his time exploring, making it his business to know every crack and crevice of his space. It did no good to think of past things. He couldn't bring his people back, no matter how hard he thought on them, nor the teacher lady who'd been kind. He was beyond emotion or explanation. He was on his own – making his own rules and his own way.

He knew little of himself other than a few stories that a Kickapoo widow woman had shared with him when he was very young. She had told him that he was from a neighboring tribe, the Keechi. His mother was a Mexican senorita and his father an Indian brave. The old woman knew not how his mother came to be with the tribe, or very much else. His father met his honorable death at the place they call Fort Boggy. Manatoa had always been curious to see this place and to know of its look. Today was as good as any day to explore and satisfy his curiosity.

He lived by his own hand, stealing what he needed and wanted, having no thought for any man. The pines in this part of the forest were tall and thick, home to many creatures' great and small. The old woman had filled his head with stories of Kickapoo legends and that was Manatoa's goal, to live as a child forever and someday catch the sun. For now, he'd stick to having fun with that white-haired pale man. He heard the white-haired man coming, with the loud mule stomping through the woods. How could one man be louder than a whole herd of buffalo? He found a perch to watch from, high above the creek below. The man and the mule stopped at the creek bed and he slid off of the beast and began rifling around in his pack. "This will be fun "Manatoa." There are four handfuls of longhorns grazing just across the creek. I will spook them and set them to run. It will be great delight to see this man run for his life."

Manatoa locked his legs around the thick branch and leaned over to reach some black walnuts on the neighboring tree. A small dead limb fell through the tree and hit the ground. The small indian did not move or even breathe. That noisy mule was kicking up a fuss now and going to spoil everything. The man led the mule across the creek up the other side. Keeping his high roost, Manatoa had filled his arms with walnuts, and he grabbed a dead piece of a limb. The fat cattle grazed and swiped their tails with annoyance at the flies and bugs that flew about. The man was looking at them with a strange gaze: surely he was not thinking he would take them home to make pets of them. "Those beasts belong to this forest and the forest belongs to Manatoa," He thought to himself with annoyance and conviction. Manatoa knew that the longhorn makes a quick trip to anger, and a shorter leap to rage. He tossed the short stick and walnuts at the large red and white marbled bull. The great beast was startled from his munching and let out a bellow of complaint. Manatoa tossed some more walnuts, hitting the animal in the head and fueling his irritation. The bull stomped at the ground setting out a charge that rippled through the whole herd. However, they were heading out the wrong way.

"What's this? A crazy man on a horse riding out among the horns? Where did he come from? He must have a wish to die today." Manatoa started to climb down from his loft when the herd suddenly spun around in their path. "What great fortune"- he thought. Their rhythmic hooves beating the ground sounded like the Nenemehkia, the powerful thunder spirits that live in the sky. It made him shudder with a tremor of fear.

The Indian boy reclaimed his spot in the tree to watch the demise of the white haired man and the crazy man riding among the horns. The pale man got the mule turned and set him to a fast trot, headed back into the creek bottom. The mule was not fast enough; the herd plowed through the creek tromping everything in its path, including the mule and the man. As the cattle were clearing the creek bottom, Manatoa eased down from the tree and went to examine the scene. He quickly scanned the location for anything of value, drawn immediately to Ollie's red bandana around his neck. He took it and the shotgun for himself as he quickly looked for knives or money.   Hearing hooves gallop to a halt, he slunked away just as the crazy man entered the creek. Sliding back into the woods, he watched to see what would happen next.

Watching carefully and making his silent observations, he paid careful attention to this one's body language and mannerisms. There was something about this man with the horse that he did not like. He knew that he could not have "fun" with this man. Not only was the rider crazy, but Manatoa felt the man wouldn't hesitate to kill him. What was that twinkle on the back of his boots? It glistened catching the reflection of the sun as he walked. "I must have a closer look" he thought.

His curiosity would have to wait, Manatoa decided to ride this one out; other than the growl in his stomach he had nowhere else to be. He slinked back to his lookout in the tree so he could follow them. When they did finally leave the following day he tracked at a safe distance, careful not to be seen or detected. He knew where they were going as he'd spied on the pale man before. This man's home was in the direction of Fort Boggy, a place he desired to see, with tricks for him to play, treasure to find, he still wanted his chicken and to catch that mysterious twinkle.

Chapter 10

By the next day, Manatoa had found him the perfect spot with shade and plenty of foliage to hide out in. He was quite good at being invisible and loved the spike of adrenaline when in the thick of a hideout. He had about decided that no one coming out of that lodge made of tree logs. He was about to make his move over to the chickens when he heard voices coming from the cabin.

He'd just have to wait a little longer. It seemed as though the crazy man was gathering supplies to do something. He came walking toward Manatoa some distance away. The little Indian thought at one point he'd been spotted, for the man looked right at him and kept walking. The glistening sun, there they were again on the heels of his boots. This would not be an easy task. He went inside the chicken house. The crazy man was talking to the birds when the best possible event happened, a rooster attack!

Manatoa struggled to stay hidden without making a sound in the thick yaupon. He stretched and bent around to watch ever so quietly as the crazy man with buckskins came dashing out of the coop, with the rooster dug in on his head. The man was running around with a rooster flogging his head! Manatoa tried hard to contain his laughter. The man was yelling at the bird while he was busily spurring him on his head. This was the most fun the little Indian had in a long while. If he could, he would have loved to compliment the man on his new hat. "That was such a great trick. I wonder if he can make the rooster do it again," he chuckled. While the man was inside the log lodge, no doubt getting mended, from the fierce warrior rooster, Manatoa walked into the coop and nabbed one of the hen sisters. There, he'd done it, just what he had set out to do! They never even saw him. It was just too easy. He almost felt bad for his neighbor.

He'd be on his way to Fort Boggy now; He had no more interest to waste on the white people. He left the homestead with the frightened hen cradled under his arm and the rifle slung over his back. He didn't really want to cook a chicken- it was never about eating the bird. It was all about stealing her. Traveling southwest when he came to the next creek, he sat the hen down on the ground and kicked at the dirt to shoo her along. She clucked, fluffed, and cackled as though she had something to complain about. He slung the rifle around and pulled it into his shoulder, pretending to shoot the bird. He'd save those few bullets he had for later. He liked the feel of the gun in his hands and the tipping of the scale in his favor; he'd never actually shot a rifle before, but he'd seen it done, and felt like he could. He grabbed a few early pecans off the ground, rolled them around in his hand, and cracked them as he resumed his steady pace again. With any luck he'd be at Fort Boggy by nightfall.

October 1845

At the cabin, Ollie recovered quickly under Sadie's watchful eye. He'd mellowed out on Ham; he hated to admit it but the ranger was kind of handy to have around. Sadie swooning over him had been annoying, but the attention to her cooking she paid was benefiting the bellies of both men. Ham didn't seem to be in a hurry to be anywhere and Ollie sure didn't mind putting this man's muscle and weight to use on the place.

Once he got over his terrible, constant headache and convinced Sadie to stop treating him like a pup, he felt like he could move about. He had plans to achieve and no more patience for lying around. Ollie's great desire was to get a barn up, or something resembling a shelter, for their dairy cow Maude. There were more traps to be set and the hog needed to be killed soon. His dream to have cattle had not died, it had only been postponed. His to-do list had multiplied just in the short time of his confinement.

Together, Ham and Ollie had hashed out the whole longhorn debacle. Ollie finally gave in and let his grudge go. Missing Old Jed had been difficult; his death was one more reminder of how much had been sacrificed to the frontier life. The two compared notes from that day, with Sadie interjecting every other thought with more questions. They had since recovered all of Ollie's tack and possessions except for his favorite red bandana and scattergun. He figured the bandana might have floated downstream, but what about the gun?   The creek had been so shallow, with not nearly enough current to relocate the gun; it should have been right there.

He and Ham had found some Indian tracks further up the creek bank, but they were faint and hard to tell if they were from that day.   What started the stampede to begin with? Neither of the men knew, and felt as though they were still missing a key factor. Ollie felt like he wasn't getting the whole story from Ham where he was going when he decided to be a hero and help.

As to the young man; he pondered the past conversations with Ham as he was shaving the bark off of the pine logs. The hot and sticky resin was of no consequence as he worked; he was glad to be out of the stuffy cabin. Should he be concerned about this "ranger" and his long walks with Sadie? Whatever his intentions were with his sister, he was still a man, no doubt one with a rugged past. The frontier hardly had enough chaperones to get to know someone properly. He knew his sister, once Sadie set her mind to something- it was like trying to count pine needles. Ollie whittled and worked on preparing the log while he pondered their friendship. He sure enjoyed this homestead. Since they arrived with Poppa, he was beginning to feel really at home and a kinship with the land. He felt renewed with hope that this whole project could really work. He and Sadie had accomplished so much in just a year's time and he wasn't about to give up on this homestead.

They needed some provisions, though, and he was in a real fix for a horse now. He could take the few pelts he'd gathered and some of the white hickory he'd chopped down to the smithy, he thought. Maybe Sadie has some handwork or jam she wants to send to Hanson's General Store that we can trade. The store keeper is not an overly talkative man but usually he is fair unless his young heathens are under foot. "It's a plan", he thought; he'd tell Sadie and Ham when they got back from their walk. First thing tomorrow, Ham and Ollie could take the wagon and head out for Alabama Ferry together. If they got an early start, they'd be back the same day and just maybe, he could find out just what Ham was avoiding.

"Heavenly Father, please meet our needs for the winter." Ollie whispered.

Chapter 11

"Thank you, Ham, for walking with me to look for pecans." Sadie said shyly as they strolled through the trees.

"Sure thing, Miss Sadie, I don't rightly mind at all. You sure can spoil a man with your home cookin'. That pecan treat you were talking about sounds real nice. It's the least I could do." Ham smiled mischievously.

"Ollie is worried that I'll wander too far, or that something will happen. He's such a worry-wart for a brother. Poppa wasn't this restricting. Oh, I know he means well. Maybe I'm a bit lonesome for company, I'm just rattling on so-"

"Nonsense, Ma'am, I enjoy hearin' someone else's thoughts for a spell. Ole Flip isn't much of a conversationalist." Ham replied and they both laughed, Ham had the water pail as they wandered the area looking for a tree to share its bounty. The wind was northerly, with a brisk gusty breeze brushing across in the limbs of the surrounding pines. The summer heat had loosed its hold with evidence of its wear on the grass and some of the trees. Ham was fixing to say something about the drought when Sadie interrupted his thought with a question.

"What made you want to become a ranger?"

Ham loved to talk about most anything except of himself, he wasn't comfortable going there just yet.

"Well, I reckon – it was on the account of-." Sadie interrupted in a loud whisper, "Shh… Ham, do you hear that?" The pair stopped in complete silence and froze, listening.

"I do hear it." Ham returned the playful look. Sadie took off at a run. "Wait!" Ham yelled as he reached out to grab her hand, but it was too late- Sadie was on the hunt. She knew exactly what that sound was; Ham started after her, following her trail in the knee-high dry grass that lay over like rippling waters.

"Mabel? Here, Mabel… come here girl!" Sadie had lost all sight of pecan hunting, her handsome walking companion, and even of her surroundings. She leapt over a fallen log, and there her hen was, huddled down looking and dreadfully lost, frightened and a bit weathered.

"Mabel, you silly hen, how in the world did you get all the way out here? You are quite a ways from the cabin: It's not like you to go so far." Sadie picked her up and caressed her fluffed feathers as she looked around, suddenly not recognizing her surroundings.

She crouched down, cuddling the hen and thinking to herself, "Ollie, is this why I can't go out by myself?" She took a deep breath and looked around. "I can do this." There was a creek just there and a good many giant oaks trees. "Wait, there is a pecan tree." She walked over, still holding Mabel, and knelt down on the ground and filled her favorite blue gingham apron pockets deep and full with the little brown treasures. She was surprised that her walking companion had not caught up with her yet; as she needed that empty pail. She filled the two pockets till the apron was dragging with a slight catch under her toe.

Standing up straight in the hen-cradled, droopy apron, with complete confusion as to her location – she began to formulate a plan. She looked at the ground, seeing the grass laid over from the direction she come. Petting the hen and reassuring herself that everything was going to be just fine, she went back in that direction to find Ham. Sadie hadn't realized just how far she'd run, and so quickly without thinking. She had heard her hen cluck and just knew it was her. She could see or hear nothing else. But, walking back a bit slower, she had time to think about just how foolish she had been. Where was that Texas Ranger when you needed him anyhow? If he couldn't track a girl and a hen in the woods how had he stayed alive this long? "Deep breaths", she coached herself. She'd need to get accustomed to the woods and finding her way back.

She followed her path and found Ham sitting on the ground leaning against a tree. She paused to look at the ruggedly handsome ranger, wearing his weathered buckskins and a slight grin on his face. She continued to reassure Mable by stroking her feathers. "Well, I declare. What happened to you?" Sadie began.

"I was chasing after this young lady with falling chestnut curls when along came this here tree. The friendly live oak invited me to sit for a spell." Ham explained. "Trees are like that, you know, real social creatures."

"How'd it do that?"-she asked inquisitively.

"I was right after you when you bolted out- and my foot hung in this here root and tripped me up. I guess I sprained my ankle, but it's not so bad, I just thought I'd sit right here and wait for you to come back. I sure am glad you came to save me, and that's definitely a first for me."

A soft rumble in the distance reminded them both they needed to be getting back soon. Sadie returned his look with a brief acknowledged glance at the clouds and a soft smile to match her enchanting eyes. "Well, while you were sitting around getting acquainted with a tree, I found the pecans I needed and my hen!" She leaned over and handed the hen to Ham, "Here, hold this."

"Wait what?" Ham held the strangely calm hen. Sadie walked away looking at the ground as though she'd lost something. She looked about and picked up a sturdy piece of oak. "She looked back at Ham and thought silently to herself, "He won't be leaving for a few more days now." She couldn't help but smile, was that so wrong of her to hope he'd stick around a little longer?

Sadie gave Ham the stick. "Well, you are too big to piggy back, and you'll have to help me find the way to the cabin." She took the hen and placed her in the empty water pail. Mabel was very cooperative and docile. She'd had a quite a trauma and was perfectly ready for her nest. Ham inched around and bore his weight on his good leg, and managed to get up. The stick had a perfect crook in the bend for his hand. While standing up trying to not bear weight on his deeply swollen ankle, he lost his balance and fell into Sadie. She was a tiny little thing with the blessing of a narrow waist and "child bearing" hips her mother so frequently told her. To her advantage, she was standing in front of the tree. Ham caught himself against, and she was unable to move.

She felt her heart beating through her chest. Surely it was so loud that he heard it also! He smelled like the open breeze, sprinkled with an aroma of leather. She loved that smell. She desired to have a love just like her parents. She believed God was going to send that man to her if she just waited patiently. Could this be him? She felt giddy with flutters in her stomach. Looking away from his captivating eyes, she grabbed the walking stick and maneuvered it about so he could transfer his weight from the tree to the stick.

He redirected her gaze and looked deep into her eyes. He took his finger and placed it under her chin to caress the softness of her face. "Pardon me, Ma'am. I seem to have lost my footing." She felt like warm butter melting right before him. Trying desperately to gather her wits, Sadie bent her knees slightly, grabbed the water pail with the hen, and her apron full of pecans. She turned out from under his arm that bore his weight against the tree. With his stick in the left hand and Sadie on the right, they limped slowly arm in arm making their way back to the cabin. Neither of them was so bold or brave to acknowledge the moment that had just transpired, as they limped along with smiles.

She grimaced and thought silently, "What will Ollie say?" Oh dear.

"Lord prepare me for the man that I am made to compliment as a helper." She thought silently.

Chapter 12

It was still dark out, with the bright glow of the full moon that allowed Ollie to get an extra early start. He'd ventured on his own at a fair distance from the cabin for hunting, trapping, and logging. Ollie was on his own for this trip, going further, and with a horse he suspected had it in for him. Fretfully he had Flip all tacked out and ready for their solo ride. Ham woke and stood, pulling himself up with the oak stick, up from his bed roll under the leanto. He hobbled around to the front porch and leaned up against the post. "Hey friend, you might want to-"

Ollie motioned with his head and a hand that he saw Ham. "Yeah, thanks I've got this all under control." While putting his boot in the stirrup he yelled over his shoulder. "I know how to ride a horse."

Ham didn't move. He was going stick around for the show. Sadie stepped out onto the porch to see him off. Ollie twisted and relaxed in the saddle. "Bye Sadie, see you tonight." Ollie shouted. As Sadie was waving goodbye, he reined Flip away from the corral. Flip exhaled a large breath, he stopped short of a whole step and shook his withers like he had a cold chill. The saddle rolled to the side, with gravity taking Ollie to the ground. Flip looked back with a toothy grin and let out a nicker while bobbing his head. They were all looking at Ollie lying on the ground; head and neck in a bind and his feet still hung in the stirrups.

"But can you stay *on* the horse?" Ham chucked with a belly laugh. "Like I was saying, you might want to walk him about and tighten up his cinch. He likes to hold his breath." Ham added.

"You might have mentioned that a bit sooner," Ollie growled. Sadie helped her brother get his feet loose from the stirrups and turn everything right side up, while Ham could be heard laughing in the background. Ollie turned back and gave his sister a big bear hug and whispered, "Thank you, and keep an eye on that one. Keep the shotgun close at all times."

She returned his look with a raised eyebrow, "Yes, I'll be just fine. I love you too." This time Ollie walked the dun horse in a circle before mounting. He kicked him hard in the flank and with a crow-hopping leap they were off as he bobbed in the saddle.

Ollie made fairly good time despite his embarrassing morning delay. He was saddled and well on his way before Capt. Crockett started his crowing. The ride was quite refreshing, with the sun coming up and the wind blowing a hot breeze out of the south. With this pace he'd arrive at Alabama Ferry sooner than he thought. He'd figured on traveling at Ole Jed pace- now realizing that Flip was the only way to travel. It was kind of that ranger fella to lend his horse, but then Ollie didn't give him much of an option. This was supposed to be a fact-finding mission on the ranger. Ham was hard to read, he kept his thoughts close, and his feelings closer. Ollie got the impression that Ham seemed unbothered by his leaving with his horse to go to Alabama Ferry Crossing.

Sadie had sent some jellies to trade and a lap quilt she'd made out of scrap material. With the furs and the white hickory that Ollie had, they just might get enough supplies to carry them through the cold months. He really needed a horse or another mule of his own, he thought. They couldn't count on the ranger sticking around much longer. Eastward he went with a steady swift trot, looking for the river. Ollie was more excited than he wanted to admit. Alabama Ferry was a small frontier town settled right at the ferry crossing. It had been months since he'd seen anyone other than Sadie and the Texas Ranger. Every time he thought of that ranger he had a cocklebur in his pants. Should he have left Sadie alone with him? What did they really know about him? It was his duty, after all, to protect her now that Poppa was gone. Deep down he didn't really feel like the man was dangerous; he'd gotten off to a rough start with the lawman. He felt that the ranger was hiding something, and that he was in no hurry to shove on for some reason. What was he avoiding?

Ollie thought as he rode, "Poppa would just about bend over backwards for his little Sadie girl. Mama always said he spoiled her so. We had ridden in that wagon for more days than we could count. In fact, Sadie and I walked most days just to not be cooped up in that rolling heap. We picked up firewood along the way, walking beside the wagon. In the evening when we stopped for supper time, we had worked up a hunger pain. Poppa had answered an advertisement by a businessman named Burnet, a speculator looking for homesteaders to make a new start on the frontier. We set out from Boston in early September of 1844, traveling through the winter, Poppa said we should pray for a mild winter and since we were going south it would be a warming up anyhow. We rested the stock and ourselves on Sundays and would read from the scriptures. We spent the day round the campfire singing hymns and stealing a nap or two. It took us all of those 6 months to get to our little piece of paradise in the pines. Rain, mud, cold, wet, and just plain miserable were most days. Mama had packed seeds away safe so we could plant a garden straight away as soon as we got here. We lost Mama and then Poppa, Ollie felt so much regret and guilt for his selfish actions.

Stepping off of the ferry, his world came back into view. He focused on the buildings lined in a row up on top of the hill. Alabama Crossing had the promise of being the next big frontier town, with the steam-boats landing and bringing in supplies from other parts of the world. The simple ferry that made travel across the river possible and commerce more abundant. As much produce went out from Hanson's new barn and granary as came in. The Antebellum Trinity College was also located there bringing people from all parts desiring an education. Settlers and wanderers of various persuasions filled the street. He could get used to this, making frequent trips to town. He had missed Boston's bustling business on every corner and street.

His trip down memory lane was trudging up day dreams of their arrival. Flip seemed to know exactly where he was going as he followed the beaten trail up the hill to the town. Ollie patted his neck gently and reassured him, "Good Boy." Flip nickered with a sense of humor Ollie wasn't sure how to interpret.

"Lord help me be frugal and wise in all my decisions." he mumbled to himself.

Chapter 13

"Hello, there?" Kershy called out as he was approaching the cabin on his bay paint mare.

Ham was sitting comfortably on the porch on a wooden chair, with his leg propped up and toes peeking out of the cotton bandage that rested on an overturned wash bucket. He made no attempt to get up. "Hello, yourself- old timer, what can I do you for?" Ham answered.

Sadie stepped into the cabin doorway and began drying the water off her hands with her apron. "I thought I heard voices. Can I help you, sir?" Sadie asked, looking puzzled.

"Sure ting, Ma'am- Me name is Kershy MacDougal. I'm vedy pleased to meet you."

"Glad to make your acquaintance. My name is Sadie Hartmann and this here is Ham; he's a Texas Ranger, What brings you out our way?"

"We be a having a church revival in these parts ma'am. Someone says, that there be settlers down this way. I weren't too sure meself. I am sure glad to find you, though. How you folks fairing these weeks?" he asked with his rich Scottish accent.

"We are doing pretty well, thank you for asking; would you like to come in for some coffee and a piece of pecan corn cake? Sadie offered.

"Aye, that be right nice of you, lassie, but I really must be on my way- I've a lot of ground to put under me feet before nightfall. The Mrs. MacDougal will have me supper, I shan't keep her a-waiting."

"Where is the revival to be, Sir," Sadie hurriedly asked.

"A small community called Raymond. It is about four miles south- as the crow flies, have ye heard of it?"

"Yes." answered Ham dryly.

"Reverend Morrell, the preaching wildcat himself, will be here for a seven-day run of preaching and singing. There'll be a tent so you won't miss it." Kershy went on. "I'm out making sure everyone in the area knows and can plan on attending. You- young lassie and your husband are both welcome to come. Oh, and the women folk will be putting on an ice cream social afterwards."

Sadie glanced over at Ham, the obvious look on his face was as priceless as hers. How would she explain this? It sure doesn't look right and that had not occurred to her till this very second. "He's not my husband,"-seeing a confused look on Kershy's face and feeling completely awkward, she went on quickly, "but well, yes, that's wonderful, we'd love to come. I'll tell my brother Ollie and we'll plan to be there. Are you sure I can't get you something before you go or for you journey on?" Sadie asked.

"No ma'am, I must be on me way. We'll see you next week then, lassie, seven days." With a last red-faced nod he turned his mare's head and trotted back the direction he came. He was a portly fellow with fair skin, red hair, and a beard to match.

"Oh how exciting, to go to a real church service, Ham, You will come with us won't you?" Sadie bubbled along grabbing a few sticks of firewood.

"I- don't know, I'm not much into church going-besides I've been here a while. I probably should be moseying on as soon as my ankle is healed."

"Say you'll at least think about it, please. What fun it would be for you, Ollie and I to go together! It will be a way for Ollie and I to say thank you for all your help you've done around here and ice cream! Won't that just be grand? Have you ever had ice cream?" Sadie just kept on pestering.

"Well no, I haven't- but you see..."

"It will be grand, oh, I hear the kettle." Sadie turned, skirts swishing to catch up, and went back into the cabin. She was humming a familiar tune. He felt like he knew it; however, he just couldn't place it. He'd love to go anywhere with Sadie. In fact, he liked her a whole bunch he was just beginning to realize just how much. The thought of leaving her made his heart pound in his chest, ache in his head, and a cold sweat form on his brow. He could abide a lot of things but church just wasn't for Ham. In fact, family and settling down wasn't for him no matter what he wanted. He needed to tell her that – he just didn't know how. He felt a twinge of pain in his shoulder; an electrifying tingle down his arm signaling the turning of the seasons and a reminder of his old wounds. He tensed his forehead and closed his eyes to breathe through the spasm. There was so much she didn't know about him. He leaned back on the wall, trying to forget; instead, the sounds of gunfire resonated and images of death played back in his mind. Regret, shame, and guilt pelted his soul, denying him the luxury of happiness. No, he just couldn't – he drew the line at playing church.

"Lord, let Ham go with us to church, and may he be blessed." she said softly as she swept the dirt floor.

Chapter 14

Ollie felt pretty pleased with himself. Aside from the mishap with the shopkeeper's boys, it had been a fine experience. Two freckle-faced versions of trouble were those Hanson boys and the two together could do some real harm someday. While Ollie and Hanson collected his list of goods, the sneaky brothers unsaddled Flip and put the saddle back on- backwards. If he had been so dense as to mount up, he'd been looking out the south end and headed for a rodeo, with that girth in the wrong place. Instead, Ollie stood there with his hands full of supplies not quite sure what to make of the scene. The farrier didn't see a thing and the horse was looking quite confused, as if he didn't know how this would work either. Embarrassed and extremely irritated, Ollie had to undo everything and start over. He even checked the saddle blankets for hidden grass burs. He remembered what Ham said this time about walking the horse so he'd exhale his breath. He sure didn't want to be dumped in the middle of town in front of all the passersby.

While he was over at Hope's Café, he was into keeping company with the kitchen maid. He tried earnestly to make conversation with the waitress. She was a doll, but clearly not too interested in Ollie's fair looks. He tried complements and polite questions to gain her attention and approval. She passed around like he was beneath her and she was far too busy to talk to him. She attended him with dry answers and a smug disposition that was not all attractive despite her figure and countenance. With no benefit of even friendship, he promptly finished his stew and coffee.

He'd seen those boys snickering and laughing as they slammed the door on their way out of the cafe. He felt them ridicule him, yet he hadn't any idea what they were up to. For sure the evidence showed up in due time. In route home his gut had a flipside purging revolt; a sudden demand to be miserable no matter where the location finds you. Someone slipped some mineral oil into his coffee, he knew without a doubt, as his mother had done the same to purge sickness from his gut. He didn't quite make it to the river, leaping off of Flip and leaving him ground-tied before he had to find some privacy in the bushes. If those boys had been anywhere near, he'd of turned them over his knee, no matter who their father was. He suspected the same little varmints, Hanson's sons- the shopkeepers boys, had a hand in his tack malfunction but he couldn't prove that either.

His investigation didn't yield much about the ranger. The farrier said he'd come through a month or so back and resupplied. Nothing in the way of details, or of his travels or dealings; good or bad. Ollie had his saddle bags full for his return trip home. He managed to get all the things on Sadie's list like saletareous, loaf sugar, chicory coffee; he even managed to get some rare wheat flour. Ollie got his crosscut saw repaired so that he could log some more trees to start building his barn. God really was blessing them. Poppa always talked about the Lord working in mysterious ways. Ollie knew that God was there, but He'd sure been awful quiet. He was feeling so heavy in his own heart.

As he crossed the ferry making his way back to the homestead, the memories were so much more real and vivid than before. Ollie felt inescapably captured now by his own regret and pain- in no way related to the intestinal purge that occurred earlier. He was always doubting his father and questioning his decisions. He felt such shame in just the admittance of the thoughts as they came to the forefront of his mind. He thought about how the Hartmann family had come so far and weathered many life storms. They were weary from travel and past ready to be on their promised land. Poppa had told Sadie to halt the wagon after crossing up the steep sandy creek embankment. It took all three of them to get Jed and the wagon up that slippery sand hill. Poppa tied the reins on the hand brake and stepped around front, he had begun to stretch his weary back as they had seen him do many times.

"Sadie, Ollie, come here-"Poppa began. "We have arrived- God has certainly blessed us with this place. We will seek to honor Him in all that we do here. Let's dedicate this property properly to him." With that declaration, Poppa unbuttoned the bottom button on his vest and knelt down on his quivering knees, praying to God as they had done many times.

Ollie had heard his Poppa pray to God his whole life, but something about this was different. He had little prickly bumps on his arms; the hair on the back of his neck was raised. He wasn't scared in any way- but more in a speechless bewilderment. His father's faith had brought them to this place. The gratitude and humbleness he saw now in his father's words and tears were beyond anything he could have imagined. In closing his prayer, Poppa stood up and gave us kids the right biggest bear hug we'd ever got, Ollie remembered. He felt such shame in that moment as he'd been resentful of his father and obstinate since Mama's passing. He wished he could have that same blind faith in God.

Right away Poppa had instructed us to pitch the tent in the rise above the creek bottom. There was a wide open spot surrounded with a hedge of pine trees up on the top of the hill from the creek bottom. Poppa said, "God has prepared this place perfect for us and tomorrow we worship God on Sunday. Now, Ollie you rest up, 'cause come Monday we'll cut some pines and get them ready to build Sadie a proper fitting cabin."

His Poppa- had pushed him to leave the life he knew in Boston behind. He'd felt like Poppa pushed this trip on his Mama. She might still be with them if they'd hadn't started out. He felt sure they could have settled over round Crockett and transferred their holdings there.

He'd felt like they should have built camp closer to the creek so they had less distance to walk. Why couldn't they take two days off instead of one? Every bit of this journey he'd fought his father, not all with words but with idle thoughts and his jeering attitude. Tears began softly falling on his face. He'd blamed his father for his mother's passing- and didn't realize it until just now. How foolish he'd been.

An old hymn his Poppa would sing began flowing through his thoughts- he couldn't remember the name. He would sing it when he was working or driving the mule team. He felt the words begin to flow again in his heart.

Just as I am, without one plea,
But that Thy blood was shed for me,
And that Thou bidst me come to Thee,
O Lamb of God, I come, I come.

Just as I am, and waiting not
To rid my soul of one dark blot,
To Thee whose blood can cleanse each spot,
O Lamb of God, I come, I come.

The words to this old familiar song he'd not heard in many weeks and months provoked a stirring in his heart. By HIS hand- God's hand had led them here. If he just could take all the resentment back! As he rode at a steady walk, the tears began to flow and he lost all sense of control. That night after they'd enjoyed a bowl of bacon and beans the three of them sat round the campfire, reminiscing about the trail; the travailing pain of the journey was already becoming a distant memory. They would sleep soundly knowing that they were finally now home.

The next morning Ollie and Sadie had waked to find their Poppa had passed on in his sleep. He was quite peaceful and content, with no stress or pain about his face. The day was somber and speechless. There was a cool spring shower for most of that afternoon. Late that evening at sunset, the pair of them stood side by side and said a final goodbye to their Poppa. The first digging of earth on their property was the burial of their father. How helpless and lonely they felt as siblings together, with no one else in the whole of the world!

Ollie felt as though the Lord was speaking to him just then as he slumped further in his seat and clung to the saddle horn, "My grace is sufficient for thee, Ollie- it's not your fault." "But God, What if they'd stayed in Boston, maybe Poppa would still be with us?" He sobbed uncontrollably. He'd not shed a tear on that day of his father's passing or any since until this moment. He knew in his heart they couldn't have stayed in Boston. Poppa believed that God had a new place for them. He believed that this eighty acres of East Texas wilderness was God's will, future, promise, and legacy for their family. His Poppa was gone but not forgotten- his legacy would continue on he must make sure of that.

"Lord, I come...blot out my sin. Forgive me Lord, I am sorry for being selfish..."

Calmness fell over Ollie as he sobbed; he gently pulled up on the reins on Flip. Just that quick, he felt the goodness of God overtake his mistakes. He pulled out his Poppa's bandana to wipe his face and blow his drippy nose. Breathing in and sighing a cleansing breath, he felt like a new man. He didn't know why he'd held on to that baggage for so long. The weight of the world had been lifted from his narrow shoulders.

"Thank You Lord, for that little talk- I'm mighty obliged. He began humming the familiar tune again, he gently kicked Flip. "Let's go home."

"Thank You Lord for forgiveness." he sighed.

Chapter 15

Manatoa's stomach was growling- he wished now he'd kept that infernal bird. His years numbered all of 13, that was his best guess- but what did it matter anyway? He had so many unknown questions. Where did his people disappear to? As much as he tried not to think about it, he did. Why did he come to live with the Kickapoo? Where were his father's people the Keechi? He felt alone and so out of place. Why did everyone always leave?

Spying on folks at Ft. Boggy would be great delight, he could plot some senseless plan to send them running in all directions. There would be animals to set free, laundry to sabotage, and cabins to raid. Manatoa laughed just thinking about it. He walked on and on in a westerly direction. It was further than he'd anticipated. He was beginning to feel dazed and limp in his arms and legs, and a strange wooziness came over him. The view of the trees before him blurred together providing a nauseating forest picture. Stopping for a short rest wouldn't be at the top of his to do list just now. He weaved and wobbled about physically, overcome with shakiness. He closed his eyes and reopened them, trying to refocus on the trees in front of him. He was realizing that his vision was still foggy and his head felt odd and heavy. Dropping to the ground, the four feet three inches of scrawny little Indian boy lay lifelessly, alone, and vulnerable in the wide-open woods.

The boy did not know how much time passed. Finally he opened his heavy eyes; they felt like he had rocks on them. He didn't want to wake up, but he struggled to keep them open. Manatoa lay still, listening to the forest noises about him. He opened his eyes just a sliver, and saw the sun shining down through the tree limbs on him; he was lying in some tall grass beneath a grandfather-sized oak tree. The limb spread of this tree was magnificent. He slowly sat up and slid over to the base of the tree to lean against it. He knew not what had happened- a strange sleep had come over him, leaving him feeling lifeless and disheveled. He felt around for the medicine pouch around his neck; it was still there. The old widow woman gave it to him for safe keeping. He opened its tiny pouch and sniffed the contents. Smelling the familiarity of his home calmed his senses and helped his composure, so he closed it up and tried to regain his bearings. He knew not the cause of his strange illness but he was ready to go on. He felt around him for the knife at his ankle. His shotgun was lying close on the ground. He must be getting close to the settlers' fort, however, he was not sure of anything at the moment.

Manatoa stood up, and the scene about him began to spin. He refocused to brace himself, trying not to get caught up in the spin. He dropped to his knees and saw a hazy figure before him, blinking his eyes with disbelief. He rubbed his face to wipe off the dirt and grime to make sure he was fully awake. Standing before him was the old widow grandmother. She looked just the same as the day he'd wandered away to the ferry village. He reached out to touch the old woman, for she was just out of his reach. He sat back on his heels and calmed himself.

"Is this a vision, Grandmother?" he asked softly.

She spoke to him softly in his native tongue. "My son, there is a battle between two wolves in us all. One wolf is evil. It is the animal of greed, anger, jealousy, resentment, inferiority, lies, and ego. The other wolf is good. He is known as joy, peace, love, hope, humility, kindness, empathy and truth. Manatoa asked, "Which wolf will win, Grandmother?"

The Grandmother replied, "The one that you feed."

He looked down at the ground to hide his tears. Braves do not cry. He had no idea why the tears were falling from his eyes; he'd never shed a tear in his whole life. He felt so alone in this part of the wood. He looked up again to ask her where their people went, and in a brief moment she was gone. He sat back against the tree with outstretched legs and continued to wipe his dirty face with a red bandana. He wanted her to come back, but just like that his mind was changed. It was time to head back to his river bottom- his home- the place he knew.   He still had no more answers about his Keechi Father than before but the burning fire in his stomach to know the truth had ceased.

On his way back to the Kickapoo shoals he should really check on the white haired man. The burn in his stomach was gone, but not his desire for trickery. There were pranks yet to plan and liberating of burdens to be done. Perhaps one day he would leave to find his people. One day he would visit this Fort Boggy. But not today. He needed to pay a visit to his neighbors on his way home. He was already formulating a plan for some sort of amusement at their expense. He was the greatest trickster in this wood, he thought, and he must maintain his reputation.

Chapter 16

Sadie was up early, putting the wheat flour to use by making biscuits for breakfast. Ollie was still sleeping and she'd not heard any movement out in the leanto. She suspected that Ollie had had a right fine trip, as he seemed lighter on his feet the evening before when he rode in. He didn't even snarl at Ham once. As she hummed the tune to her favorite hymn, she had to admit that she had been enjoying the company of Mr. Abner; even if it was for a short time. Those dark eyes and blocky chin had swept her heart away. She listened for the thud of Ham's his boots and the jingle of the spurs on the porch.

"Sadie, - earth to Sadie, girl?" Ollie said again, interrupting her dreamy gaze. Ollie was sitting on the side of his bed scratching his head, trying to figure out her daze.

"Yes, brother, you need some coffee?" she shot him a quelling look.

"Well, sure- if you're a-pouring, what's got you smiling so early in the morning?"

"Oh nothing special, I wanted to put this flour to use that you brought home. It will go special with my blackberry jam. Do you think that Mr. Ham will like that?" Sadie inquired.

"Hmm, it's likely; he's liked everything else you put in front of him so far," Ollie muttered with a half bite of sarcasm. "I'll go out and feed the chickens, check on Flip, and the hog. I'll leave Maude for you to milk. She's pretty fussy lately and you girls no doubt will have plenty to talk about. I would imagine that ranger's time is counting down- maybe if he gets over his bum leg he could help us slaughter the pig before he gets back on his way." Ollie stood up with a thud as his heels sank into his boots. He pulled up the salmon-colored suspenders over his shoulders and smoothed his cotton-top cow lick on the back of his head. She really did have a pretty fantastic brother, Sadie thought. She smiled contently and then thought through what Ollie had just said.

Sadie caught Ollie's attention as he was headed for the door, "Wait? Back on his way? Ham is leaving? He hasn't said anything to me." Sadie's heart began racing and she was almost in a panic. She dropped the wooden spoon on the floor and knocked over a cup of water, sending a mess across the floured table.

"Whoa- easy, No, He's not said anything, but I spect he'll be wanting to get on his way soon." Ollie answered directly while grabbing his worn-out hat off of the peg by the door. Sadie knew it would be forward of her to ask him to stay; she wasn't raised like that. "Deep breathe in and out," she coaxed. "He doesn't even have a home," she thought to herself as she heard the door latch thud.

"Lord I put this in your hands." She said in a gentle whisper as she wiped up the mess on the table.

Headed out the cabin door, Ollie exchanged pleasantries with Ham. Sadie's heart jumped a little as she heard them talking. Instantly her mood changed from gloom to glee. She quickly cleaned up the mess she'd just made. The two men talked of the weather, the critters, and the smell wafting from the kitchen in the cabin. Finally parting they both agreed on each other's morning reports.

"Good Morning, Sadie, I smell something frightfully good." Ham entered the cabin cheerfully. He hobbled in with his makeshift cane that Sadie had found for him. He reached out with the other hand and grabbed the back of the chair plopping himself down and elevating his foot. Wiggling his toes, he made a show of his dingy grey sock that had a hole on the right side of the big toe and another started on the heel.

"Thank You, How are we feeling this morning?" Sadie inquired.

"Feeling mighty good for an ole ranger."

"You aren't so old."

"I'm not young either. Another day or so and I'll be ready to ride."

"Ride?" Sadie replied with confused glance. She stopped short of the table, taken in a bit sudden by his statement.

"I'd like to learn to ride." Sadie tried to divert the conversation.

"You've never been riding?" Ham asked.

"No, not a horse. Poppa, let me set on the mule and led me around while we were resting on a Sundays. Mama, said it weren't proper for a lady to ride. But Poppa had said he'd teach me soon as we got settled here, as we all needed to learn new things."

"Well, yes ma'am, I reckon I could manage that task, if you promise to listen well and not take off on a whim."

"Take off on a whim?" Sadie snapped, while flipping the salt pork in the skillet and throwing him a confused glance. "What do you mean by that?"

"Remember the chicken?" Ham said plainly. She gave a half grin, with her smile lines creased the way he liked. Her playful attitude and rambunctious spirit coupled with her sweet innocence was quite attractive. "Soon as my ankle heals, Flip and I really need to get back on the trail. Your brother is all healed and doing just fine. It's rumored that Texas will join the Union. If that's the case, I may be needed elsewhere. I need to check in with Captain Hayes and get my new station."

Sadie paused, holding the metal plates and a fork pointed at him as though it were loaded. "Do me this favor Ham, would you?" She looked at him serious with pleading eyes. "Don't leave until you let me darn those dingy socks for you."

"Is that all?"

"Well, you could go to the tent revival with Ollie and me. It would mean so much to both of us."

"Is that a threat?" She sure was adorable when she was being serious! Those green eyes started glowing and pointed straight at his heart.

"A threat- what do you mean?" Sadie retreated.

"You look pretty threatening with that fork in your hand. You really should point that in a safe direction." Ham laughed the conversation off.

She moved about trying to be calm and keep her emotions in check. She was being serious. How did he rile her up so quickly? She set the table with napkins, plates, and forks, shifting pieces about the table to make room for the hot dishes to come.

"Would you call Ollie in?" Sadie requested.

Ham shifted in the chair and tried to verbalize his plight. "I'm not much of the church going type, Sadie." He stated. He wanted to confide in her and tell his whole story- how his life had been riddled with loss and death. How could he be honest with her? There was so much to atone for. He didn't deserve the attention or love that this friendship could afford. She deserved a better man. If she knew where he'd been, she would turn on him, just like God. He could ride out of here and this interval would join all the silent memories in his mind. He nervously picked up the fork and began tapping the table.

"I....should" Ham started.

"I realize that, but Ollie and I are so grateful for your help, and we would like for you to go and celebrate with us." Sadie interrupted. "It's just one service, and if it weren't for you, my Ollie would not be with us."

Why did she have to be so persuasive? The better question was, why couldn't he tell her no? Laying the fork down and taking a deep breath, "If it means that much to you, I reckon I can stay on for that." Ham conceded.

The cabin door swung open wide and Ollie came in, carrying eggs and a pail of fresh water. "Isn't that right, Ollie?" Sadie quizzed.

"Sure thing, what did I just agree too, Ham?

"It's of no use, Whitey, I don't think we will win." Ham gave in. "And the food is ready."

"Well, that's settled! You *are* going with us, and I'll hear nothing else about it. Breakfast is ready, guys, and I hope you're hungry- I might have made a feast," Sadie said happily. The three sat down to the table and joined hands. Ollie offered the blessing and the thanks for the day. How blessed Sadie felt right at this particular moment to have her brother on one side and the man that her heart beat for on the other. If life could just stay this perfect, that would be fine by her.

"Wait, did you just call me Whitey?" Ollie asked.

"God Bless this trip." Sadie thought as smiled to herself.

Chapter 17

The last real service Sadie had attended with her Mama and her Poppa was back before they left Boston to come south. She was feeling a mite emotional over that fact and all aflutter with the thought of spending the day with Ham. She found time to slip away to the creek and use the lilac water that was her Mama's, and she'd washed and ironed her best frock. It had been months since she felt like she had a need or reason to fix up. She had put a little lard in her curls to tame the frizz, and she found a pretty red ribbon to tie at the end of her plaited hair, twisting it into a bun. She'd also prepared a picnic lunch for them of some leftover fried salt pork, hard boiled eggs, and pecan bread.

"What's wrong with you, Sadie Hartmann?" she thought silently to herself. She was obviously so nervous, excited, and scared all that the same time, like a fifteen-year-old school girl going to the Stoney's Annual Harvest festival. She was not a little girl anymore. Cresting twenty years and living on the frontier had aged her face with a tan but not changed her innocence. She emerged from the cabin arms laden with her bonnet, picnic baskets, and her Poppa's familiar family Bible tucked safe under her arm.

"Hey there, let me help you," Ham came over quickly from the wagon.

"Where's your stick?" Sadie noticed right away.

"No need for it." Ham praised. His ankle had healed quickly and didn't need the walking stick any longer. He was clean shaven and smelled as though he had a bath at the creek. His buckskins seemed strangely freshened. He reached over to grab the picnic basket and his eyes met with Sadie's. The pair seemed lost in their gaze for a split second.

"Let me take that for you." Ham reached out to grab the load she bore to the wagon. Smiling she said nothing- but allowed him to be a gentleman.

"You wait right there." Ham ordered. Sadie curtsied and stood waiting for her escort to return.

Ham reached out for her hand and complemented on the loveliness of her gown and appearance. She felt color warm her cheeks as she returned the admiring remarks to his improved appearance.

"Well, are we a going?" Growing impatient, Ollie piped up, prompting an increase in the speed of his passengers. The sound of Ollie's voice returned their gaze to reality. Ham spun on his heels offering his arm as an open invitation to escort Sadie to the wagon. She returned his gesture, resting her arm in his and grabbing her skirts to step down from the porch. She delicately put her arm in his for the short walk toward Ollie and the wagon. Ham felt a strange churn in the pit of his stomach, similar to the day of his arrival. It was not like a sickly sour-milk feeling; it was more like getting to work with a newborn foal kind of excitement. He set the wooden block down for Sadie to step up into the back of the buckboard.

"Its real fine of you to use your horse to pull our wagon so we can all go to the service," Sadie said, while tying her bonnet on and arranging her skirts.

"About that, Sadie, I'm not a real churchy kind of feller. I've done some things that I'm not real proud of. I don't want you to get any wrong ideas." Ham struggled to get the words out.

"Nothing you've done can be *that* bad," Sadie responded. Ham's face seemed so burdened and stressed as he walked up to check the rigging on Flip. This was one of those moments he wished he and Flip were hot on the trail of some wild-eyed vaquero. He felt a strange tug to pull and leave that he could not explain.

There was no road to Raymond, just a path through the woods, curving and winding to avoid the sand pits and overgrown thickets with briars. Halfway into the wagon ride, as they moved slowly through the pines, the sky began to turn a dark threatening blue. They desperately needed rain to quench this hot summer earth but no one was interested in being a duck out in it. Hit and miss, water droplets the size of blueberries began to fall. Ham was so focused in on driving Flip; he hardly seemed to notice the moisture drizzling down on them. He was immersed in some deep thought. Sadie and Ollie were enjoying themselves with conversation reminiscing about Poppa and Mama attending meetings back east.

"Do you remember the time Mama got in a fuss with Mrs. Witerson? " Sadie asked.

"Who?"

"You know Mrs. Witerson, the organist. She was the absurd young widow that was in love with the Parson. Everyone knew except the widow and the young preacher. Mama got in a fuss with her over the inefficiency of her organ playing."

"Ah, yes, I remember now." Ollie shook his head with a wide smile. Their Mama, Mrs. Hartmann, was a perfectionist, a no-nonsense woman with a stiff straight back and German heritage. Mama didn't play the organ. That petty fact was irrelevant to the problem; Mama had told Mrs. Witerson in so many words what she thought of *her* lack of musical talent. Poppa, being the positive peacemaker, had scolded Mama and encouraged her to make it right, as we shouldn't criticize someone serving the Lord. Mama argued with Poppa that Mrs. Witerson wasn't serving the Lord, but trying to impress the Pastor and doing a poor job at it. Mama said, "Our ears begged for mercy when we had to endure her playing each and every service."

Mama gave in and made a carrot cake with a dry apology to deliver to Mrs. Witerson. Poppa said, "It was true- it didn't matter if she couldn't carry a tune in the warsh pail or not, she was serving the Lord so we ought not to be a-judging her." We had a great laugh, Sadie remembered, because her organ playing *was* really that bad, Mama just called it like it was.

Ham pulled up on the reins and brought Flip to a halt, taking in the view of the brown, thirsty pastures and fabulous large oaks, elms, and hackberry's, with leaves beginning to take a turn preparing for fall. Ollie announced loudly with excitement, "Sadie, Look here- we've arrived." Bending around trying to see from her spot in the back of the wagon, there was so much to take in. Sadie thought.

"The old feller Kershy was right, there is no way you could miss that tent- that's the biggest tent I ever saw." Ham said, with a hit of sarcasm. "Look at all the bonnets," Ollie commented with interest.

"Lord, bless this service." Sadie thought silently.

Chapter 18

Ham found a shade tree some distance away from the tent to tether Flip to and promptly loosed his rigging. Sadie and Ollie looked about, making acquaintances and hoping to find their host. Raymond was nothing more than a small family community. There was no post office, no trading post, or even a blacksmith, just a community of a few families that nestled together all in one area. Sadie had no idea that there were quite so many settlers in this part of the woods. The women had congregated where the eating tables were set up, a short distance behind the tent area. Boys and girls ran and played, tagging each other with animation and energy. Kershy wasn't too hard to locate. His red hair and beard with rosy red cheeks stood out among all the other men while his hearty belly laugh and friendly disposition made him everyone's favorite conversationalist. Mrs. MacDougal was quite as fair, and of similar proportions. She was an accomplished cook and wore a long face, and sharp eye for her wild red-haired daughters. She seems a gracious hostess, and poured up some refreshing lemonade to quench their thirst from traveling.

Sadie and Ollie made their introductions. The MacDougal's had three daughters, each as fair as the other. The eldest, Alison- known to her friends as Ali, took an eye right quick to Ollie. While Ollie was making his acquaintance with young Ali, Sadie excused herself to take Ham some lemonade.

She found him, rechecking and over checking the tack on Flip. "Here is some lemonade, Ham."

"Thank you, right kind of you, Sadie."

"Are you all right? You were awfully quiet on the way here. Is there something bothering you?" Sadie asked.

Ham didn't know where or just how to begin. He knew for sure that God didn't want him; that was apparent already. And as soon as Sadie figured that out she wouldn't want him either. If he could just make it through this service, and take Ollie and Sadie home, he and Flip could be on their way. He'd done far worse things than sit through a service before. Then he'd be on his way with no looking back, just putting those green eyes and chestnut curls behind him, as a fond memory of the past. Those sweet smile lines and soft delicate hands would soon be just part of his history. "Yes, Sadie, I'm fine. Is it time for the meeting? Where's your brother?

"I believe so-He'll meet us over there, but if you need talk about something- seems like something is bothering you?"

"I'm right as rain- just like this rain in fact, that keeps trying to fall. Come on now Sadie girl, you've got a revival meeting to attend." He forced a smile as he turned and patted Flip on the rear. He reached out to extend his arm to Sadie for the walk over to the tent. The tent was massive, and it was full of wooden benches lined in rows. The men of the community had constructed a small stage area for the parson to stand on. The two found a seat three-quarters of the way back toward the side. They sat further away from the crowd and close to the edge of the tent for easy exit. Ollie joined them just as the music began, and Sadie slid over to make room for Ollie to sit in between herself and Ham.

Ham scanned the crowd and those standing on the edges. He couldn't help but look for potential trouble. Readjusting his gun belt, he sat uncomfortably on the bench. Feeling his arm twinge with a reminder of the pain and wounds he bore. He rolled his shoulder as he adjusted himself on the wood bench to hide the involuntary twitches in his arm.

Kershy was a man of many talents apparently. He was leading the congregation in hymn or two before the speaker began. Ham heaved a large sigh and thought to himself, "This isn't so bad- I can do this."

Then Wildcat Morrell took the wooden stage. His notoriety and popularity had preceded him. He was known well in this area as "a tell it like it is, hell-fire, and brimstone preacher." He rode on horseback from village to village, preaching God's word and planting churches all over central and east Texas. He was a broad-chested man with a tall inseam, a bushy gray beard and dark hair with a hint of gray beginning to appear. His booming voice carried the length and breadth of the tent. As he spoke words which were heavy with conviction and divine authority.

As the preacher boldly delivered the word, Ham became increasingly uncomfortable. The bench was hard, his ankle was now throbbing, his arm twitched, *and* the deteriorating weather distracted him. He sat and tussled within himself until the end of the sermon. This had been a bad idea. He slid out the side of the tent to excuse himself as if nature was calling. Instead his nervous jitters brought him to check on Flip. He mind was reeling; what did God expect of him? He desperately needed to get away. As he busied his hands making ready for the journey home, a voice startled him.

"Ham, are you all right, son?" Kershy inquired.

"Yes sir, I needed to get up and move around. Sorry if I disturbed anyone, "Ham apologized, as he rubbed his arm and shoulder to ease the random spasms he felt.

"Son, Forgive me for saying so, I believe that God is dealing with you: He will forgive anything we've done. Can I pray with you?" Kershy questioned.

"That's just the thing- I know I'm a sinner, I'm not asking for God's forgiveness, I know I've done wrong. I was doing just fine on my own," Ham snapped turned toward Kershy in anger.

Flip, sensing Hams frustration, let out a snort and stamped his front feet. The loose bridle came undone and fell down across his nose. He bobbed his head to show his disfavor of the leather bridle. Turning his attention back to his horse, he picked up the bridle and adjusted the blinders, fastening them.

"How true that is, son, but God doesn't want you walking around through life carrying all that baggage. Let Him help you with the load; He can give you the forgiveness you're looking for." Kershy stepped forward and stood, resting his hand on Flip.

Ham bowed his head and said softly with shame in his voice, "Can God forgive me for what I've done- Have I gone too far? I have killed men. No, I don't think so." Looking up, he met Kershey's eyes. "No, I will not be praying, nor will I need your prayers. Thank you kindly for the invitation but as soon as the Hartmann's are ready, we will be on our way."

Ham finished getting Flip ready and pulled the wagon up to the front, waiting for his passengers. Sadie hadn't seen Ham since before the service ended. She saw him setting in the wagon, looking heavy and burdened.

She got the distinct feeling that it was time to go, so she walked around and found Ollie; he was over at the MacDougal's table, talking to their daughter Alison. Sadie went over to pay her thanks and appreciations, and to urge Ollie over to the wagon. Mrs. MacDougal insisted that they each take a serving of ice cream; she assured them they'd never tasted anything quite so heavenly in all their years.

Just before Ollie walked away, a very serious Kershy pulled him to the side for a private word. Sadie wasn't sure what the trouble was. Kershy was such an easy to get along with fellow, but now his face was somber and serious; maybe it had something to do with his young Aly talking to Ollie.

The teasing thunder finally gave into its need to rain. The dark blue cumulus clouds let go of their liquid burden, not just some random blueberry sized droplets but a heavy straight-down drenching pour to quench the thirst of the ground. The rain sent the settlers running for cover, grabbing up food and dishes off the tables and heading for the large tent enclosure. Sadie and Ollie made their way to the wagon where Ham was just sitting, with water running off of his hat and trailing off of the fringe from his buckskins.

"Are you alright?" Sadie shouted in the rain. "Do you reckon we should wait a bit for the storm to pass before we head home?"

"No, I think we should ride on. We are already wet and Flip doesn't spook easily. We best be going before it gets any later." Ollie helped Sadie into the back of the wagon and he took his place next to Ham up front. She had stuffed the family Bible down in her dress to save it from getting too wet. The siblings made no argument or fuss; they had gathered their things and loaded up for the journey back. Sadie was sad to be leaving quite so soon but had felt the anguish in Ham's spirit as he fled the tent. She watched the big tent and the settlers fade into the distance as they rode away, jiggling from the bumpy terrain.

"Lord thank you for this service and please comfort Ham." She whispered.

Chapter 19

The wagon ride home was anything but silent. Minus the soft patter of rain, Ollie couldn't stop talking about the red-haired beauty that had already stolen his heart. He was delighted by the offer that Kershy had made for him to come and work on his homestead. As payment for helping Kershy with some building improvements to his property, Ollie would get a horse! Not just any horse, a mountain bred stock horse that would be perfect for working in the gullies and creek bottoms.

"That's such a blessing, right, Ham?" Sadie tried to awaken him from his thoughts.

"Yeah, what's that?" Ham answered, confused. His thoughts were jumbled, dull, and coarse. He was struggling to make sense of the past, the sermon, and his impending future. The best scenario was for him to keep to himself and not say too much, for fear of literally saying *too* much.

"Kershy is letting Ollie work for a horse; don't you think that is a blessing?" Sadie said with excitement. Ham was being so quiet and Sadie wanted to do whatever she could to ease his mind. It bothered her to see him dealing with this issue whatever it was. If he would just open up to her! Well, she had to admit she didn't know *what* he needed. She prayed softly in her mind. *"Dear Lord, please help Ham with whatever is ailing him."*

"Sure thing, Miss Sadie, that's real good." Ham answered without smiling maintaining his stoic presence.

Clearly Ham had something weighing heavy on his mind. He didn't say much more going back to the cabin than he said on the way to the revival. The trip back home seemed half as far as going, maybe because they were more relaxed and had less anticipation for the day. Sadie wasn't sure but it seemed like even Flip was a bit antsy to get back as well.

It was after dusk when they pulled up into the familiar farm yard they'd left that morning. All of them were famished and hungry; they'd not had time to eat their picnic in the urgency to get home. They had been gone just the duration of the day, but Sadie missed the familiar place that had grown to feel like home. She hadn't realized just how much it felt like home until this moment! Ollie hopped off of the wagon before it stopped to go check on the hog and Maude, the milk cow. While Sadie gathered her wet bonnet and other soggy items to carry in, Ham halted Flip in front of the cabin. After looping the reins on the hand brake, he shook his arm as though to relieve some unseen tension. He stepped down off of the wagon, careful of jolting his ankle but in haste to assist Sadie. Grabbing the wooden block, he slid it toward him at the edge of the wagon, and dropped it with a roll beneath the wagon edge. Ham held his hand out to provide support for Sadie as she stepped down out of the wagon, absorbing every second of time he had left with her sweet, angelic face. With both arms full, Sadie stepped out with blind faith and missed the block step entirely. She stepped into thin air and fell backward just almost into the wagon. Ham instinctively swooped with his left hand down, quickly wrapping it under her legs with the other arm around her back to catch her just before she fell against the edge of the wagon.

Catching her breath, swallowing deep, she looked straight into those dark eyes, "Thank You- sir. That was close. I am indeed in your debt."

"You are most welcome". Ham responded flatly. As he set her feet firmly on the ground, Sadie was feeling flushed and slightly embarrassed. Her heart still racing, and feeling all out of character with her droopy rain-wet hair, Sadie stood and straightened her saturated dress. "I'm going to put on some coffee, to warm us up. Would you like a cup?" she said as she looked at Ham with such a sweet innocent face, blinking those beautiful long eyelashes.

"Yes' m I believe so."

Ham turned and went straight for Flip and led him to the hitching post at the corral. He began loosening the rigging on his horse as once again his stomach churned. Sadie couldn't be sure if it was rain or if Ham had tears on his face. It was hard to see, even on the moonlight night as the moon was hiding in and about the clouds. Whatever was eating at this ranger, it was time for her to get to the bottom of it. She just knew that this outing together would be what they needed. She didn't want to lose Ham Sadie thought; she felt like she'd lost so much already. She already loved everything about him, the sway in his walk, the blockiness of his chin, his sincere willingness to help, and the kindness that hid under his rough exterior. The thought of him leaving was too much. She needed to share her heart and she needed to do it tonight.

"Lord give me the courage to speak my heart," she *spoke softly.*

Chapter 20

"Friend, are you going somewhere tonight? Ollie asked, as Ham was now saddling and bridling Flip.

"Yes, it's time I was a moving on." Ham answered dryly.

"Have you talked to Sadie about this? Can't it wait till morning?"

"No, I haven't but, it doesn't matter, it's all the same. It's time I am heading out, you are all healed up and doing just fine. My debt to you is square. Do me a favor and don't go rounding up anymore longhorns by yourself." Ham threw Ollie a quick and joking glance. "My ankle is better and well, it's just time. I need to go before something else breaks loose."

"Like what, what are you not saying, Ham?" Ollie demanded. "Come on now, you don't have to leave this way; soaked to the bone and at night. What are you running from?"

Ham now was a mite perturbed at Ollie's persistence. "It's none of your concern, and I'd lower my voice and take two steps back if I were you, friend." Ham was standing firm, face to face with his hand resting on his gun. Ollie had never seen this side of Ham. In a quick reflex, Ollie took a step back with a confused look. "I should have checked in with Capt. Hayes by now, is all there is to it." Ham finished, taking a deep breath and turning back to his horse.

"Don't try to stand in my way. Trust me, this is for the best," he reiterated.

"The best for whom? Listen, I know we got off to a rough start with the stampede in all. I haven't exactly been welcoming. I was wrong, and I see that now. You were just trying to help. You are going to crush my sister this way. Stay around another day or two and help me figure all this out. I don't think my shotgun just floated down the shallow creek on its own, nor did Sadie's hen just go for a stroll in the woods."

Ham turned from his horse and looked at Ollie intensely, as if he was fixing to unleash a cussing that even Crockett would be fond of. He caught himself before opening his mouth he wasn't thinking clearly and he knew it.

Sadie walked out onto the porch with a cup of coffee in one hand and small black lantern in the other. The light was soft around her face; she'd changed into a dry work dress and her curls hung long on her back, still damp but with spiral perfection.

"What's goin' on?" Sadie addressed the two, not understanding what she was seeing.

Ham turned Flip in a quick circle, put his left foot in the stirrup and slung his leg quickly over the saddle. Flip began to prance in place while Ham adjusted himself in the creaking leather saddle.

Sadie stepped forward, closer to Ham and Flip. "You have your bed roll and all your things? Are you leaving?" Sadie questioned as she was lifting the light to look more clearly. She wanted to see the expression in his face.

Ollie moved closer to his sister to console her as he knew that the ranger was indeed leaving, and that reality was becoming clearer for her. Her brother reached out to take the lantern from her hand. Ham rode closer to her; he leaned down from the high perch in the saddle and nuzzled closer to her face. "Sadie girl, I'm sorry. I have to go. I'm not the man you deserve."

"When will you be back?" Sadie pressed for an answer while tears began to form in her eyes. She wasn't sure what was happening. Her heart was beating impatiently and she was unsure if an altercation had just taken place with her brother, or if she was to blame.

"Just know that I love you." Flip was now prancing in circles, feeling the emotions of the two. Ham pulled back on the reins and commanded Flip to "Stand". Flip stamped his feet settling into a false sense of calm. Ham leaned in for a soft sweet kiss, and her lips met his with exquisite bliss. He tasted the wet salty tears from her face, feeling that he'd never experienced anything so wonderfully passionate and with so much pain at the same time. That would be the last moment he remembered of his sweet Sadie girl. He hadn't expected to fall for this woman. In his mind he tried to rationalize that he could stay, but he knew the facts of his life and he must spare himself the loss. Knowing this was the right thing to do didn't make it any easier. He had to leave; there could be no attachment for him, he reminded himself, although it was agony in his heart. He felt like he had been shot with a poison arrow straight through the chest; in fact that would have been less painful.

"Lord, I don't understand, please give me strength." She thought to herself as her brother comforted her with a warm hug.

Chapter 21

Riding out of the clearing Ham felt as though he was leaving a piece of himself behind. His face burned with conviction and guilt. The rain clouds had long cleared out and the harvest moon was a full bright orange, hanging above the trees at his back. His clothes were soaked to the bone but that hadn't mattered. It had been a month since he'd arrived there at this little paradise in the pines. He'd never forget that day she came running from afar and he'd lost his words right out of his head. The mere sight of her rendered him speechless but there was no place for Sadie girl in his life.

"That preacher was wrong; he didn't know anything about me. I am what I made of myself." Ham thought aloud. This was his legacy, a lineage of death and loss. Ham's father, Henry had died in the war of 1812; he was a soldier who went with other soldiers from their state to provide reinforcements in Washington. He was among the casualties when the British invaded and burned down the capital. Ham's dear mother, Louisa, was a school teacher in Tennessee, where their people were from. She caught a deadly case of pneumonia a couple of years after his birth. Ham was but a young boy, sent to live with his paternal grandparents in South Carolina. Ham's Grand pappy and Grams were the closest relationship to parents that he remembered. They owned a horse ranch, raising thoroughbred stock horses to supply the American soldiers. The spread was a modest ranch of 200 acres where Ham got all the time on the back of a horse he wanted, and all the fresh air a boy could breathe.

From there life seemed to snowball downhill. The passing of his grandparent's one at a time was hard to handle. The family ranch fell into foreclosure, with the bank leaving him with nothing - no inheritance, no home, no family, and no future there. There was nothing to keep him tied down to South Carolina and there was no one left in Tennessee. Ham read of an advertisement where they were looking for young men with no families. He inquired and promptly joined up with the rangers to run from it all.

Rangerin' suited him, keeping with his theme that if there were no attachment there can be no heartache. No friends and no family equaled no death or loss in his mind, and that was the way he rode. Wildcat Morrell had no business telling me that I'm a sinner. I know I've done bad things, but I don't need his judgement too. Riding hard, headed west, Ham pushed himself and his horse. He looked at the stars and shouted aloud. "I'm not supposed to be alive, God! Do you hear me? I was there. I was at Coleto Creek-Where were you? I should be dead with all my brothers. Why didn't you take me too?" He petitioned God, waiting for an audible answer, kicking harder into Flip's flank, he pushed him to go further and faster. His thoughts went back…

Colonel Fannin insisted on pushing on even though the stock needed a rest. Being pushed to their limits they were hungry and tired, and the supply wagon was broke. We were forced to camp in the middle of the day in a field by Coleto Creek. We saw them Mexicans coming from afar at a full-out gallop. They surrounded us before we could make for a better position in the trees. There was nowhere to hide or retreat to, so we just stayed in formation and *shot* it out. If we tried to bolt we were picked off, one at a time. Jesse and I hunkered down behind some overturned wagons and worked to pick off their targets. Jesse, his Tejano friend from was wounded in the arm but continued to fight. Despite the blood that covered his shirt, Ham managed to patch up Jesse's arm with a makeshift tourniquet. However, that would not be enough; a rogue bullet made impact, quickly ending his life. Jesse's passing was so sudden; Ham remembered how difficult it had been to accept.

On the following day, the Mexicans had received reinforcements. Col. Fannin promptly surrendered to them to save his men from further loss of life. They checked everyone and took the survivors back, Ham recollected, to La Presidia Baha and held us captive in a chapel for days, those with serious injuries they shot immediately on the site. It was *so* hot, and they refused us doctoring or freshwater. I knew that they were not going to let us go.

It seemed at first that I might have been wrong. There was talk of the Mexicans releasing us. A band of soldiers took a group of us Texians out, leaving Col. Fannin and the others behind. The Mexican army marched us a mile or so from the camp. We were all so excited to see the sun and breathe the fresh air after being holed up in that sultry church for days! Men were talking about seeing their wives and children again. They discussed their plans for returning home and pursuing their farming or ranching. Our captors walked with a smile and even laughed as well. Had this war come to an end? Were we being released?

They marched us to a shallow ravine, ordering us to line up shoulder to shoulder. They lined up the same and took aim with their rifles and shot. We were brought out to be shot by a firing squad; we weren't being released! I was shot in my right shoulder. The bullet went clean through, leaving a hole in its path. When I hit the ground I must have hit the back of my head on a rock, *and* it knocked me out. When I came to, the soldiers had left us for the buzzards. My brothers-in-arms all lay around me dead; I could not see another living soul. I ripped what was left from my shirt and tried to bandage myself. The right side of my body was heavy and cumbersome, in excruciating pain, but there was no time to stop, and wait. I had no strength to grip with my right hand, I felt a fever coming on. Under the cover of night, I walked out of there in search of help.

I found shelter in a home not far away as I was trying to make my way back to General Houston. A couple loyal to the freedom of Texas patched me up and hid me in a barn for three days. The man's wife applied herb poultices to my wounds to draw out the infection. I needed to rest longer, but I was afraid of putting them in jeopardy. They gave me a burro and provisions to make my way back to General Houston. After many days travel, weak and weary, I finally arrived and told him of our ill fate. The General had already received word and was planning a retaliation. He told me I shouldn't have any regret, but my conscience would not let me off so easily. I gave no thought of those I'd killed in battle; but for those that lay behind and were still held captive, I felt responsible, and still do, Ham brooded. I bear such guilt. I shouldn't be alive. I should have died with my brothers. God, why didn't you take me too!?

Ham had ridden hard all night, reliving his past in his mind. He stopped at the Navasota River, knowing that Flip was spent and needed rest. Ham slid off of the saddle to the muddy earth of the river bank and cried his heart out. He held his shoulder tight to his body to mute the pulsing throbs of pain. "I give up- I can't do this anymore- help me God! Take this burden from my soul!" Feeling emotionally spent, flushed, and dizzy with fever. Ham couldn't fight any longer.

"Dear God, if you are out there, I know I've done wrong. Forgive me for fleeing my brothers; I know I'm a sinner. I am so sorry. I do believe on your son, Jesus Christ. I believe what that preacher said that he died for

me on the cross and that He rose again the third day and now Jesus is alive in heaven with you. That preacher said- He was coming back for us. Can you put me on that list? God, please forgive me of my sin and shame-- come into my heart. I want peace in my life and I just can't fight and run anymore. –Uh, Thank You, In Jesus name, AMEN."

Immediately Ham felt such a peace wash over him that he'd never felt in his whole life. In all his years he'd never felt this clean- this forgiven.

"Thank You God." He said, in his mind as he drifted off.

Chapter 22

Thinking it over, Manatoa wasn't sure really what happened. Quietly tracking his way back to the shoals, he wore his new favorite red bandana around his neck and the shotgun slung over his back. He knew he'd had a vision of the old grandmother. Visions were most important, and not to be taken lightly. He felt strangely renewed and invigorated. Exploring Fort Boggy would have to wait a little while longer. He didn't need to invite white men with guns to come looking for him just yet.

He refreshed himself at the creek and munched on some wild onions. Sitting perfectly still under the tree, he watched the squirrels run while collecting nuts. One brown squirrel kept coming closer and closer; Manatoa couldn't help the tempting notion that popped into his head. He'd gathered a lapful of pecans and leaned back flat on the ground beneath the tree. Time was of no consequence as he closed his eyes and pretended to doze off. Waiting patiently, he slowed his breathing, and became still, becoming one with the tree and the earth beneath him. The greedy squirrel ventured closer and closer to Manatoa, then scurried off quickly and added more nuts to his pile, scrambling up the tree and back down. Then he paused and sat watching for Manatoa to move. When he did not even so much as breathe, the little nut gatherer ventured even closer. He was so close now that he was sitting right beside the Indian boy's leg, holding a pecan from his lap. The boy cracked open one eye just to see him. As the squirrel sensed his movement, he sought to break and run up the tree. Manatoa grabbed him by the tail, sending a shrieking noise rippling through the woods. All the other critters vanished with the brown squirrel nabbed in a hysterical panic. The boy had caught his prize and he put him in his small carry sack. He would save him for later. Feeling refreshed and accomplished Manatoa slung the bag over his shoulder and set back on his journey.

He was almost to the lodge of the white-haired man. He would sneak about and see what he could see. The fire was out in his stomach but not his love for stealing and trickery. There were still pranks to play and mischief to be thought up and accomplished.

Nearing the cabin, Manatoa he saw the wagon tracks going away into the woods. He bent down and touched his hand to the ruts and determined the wagon had been gone awhile. That evidence had him intrigued already. Further into the homestead he crept, bare footed, silent, looking, and waiting. He found a spot in the yaupon where he could lurk without being seen, listening for noise from the cabin. It was strange; he heard absolutely nothing. Manatoa felt something hard poking the ball of his foot. He reached down for a closer look and found a broken piece of antler with a pointed end and a very sharp blunt end on the side of the break. Sliding it safely in his pouch with the squirrel, he sat motionless and resumed his concentration again.

As it grew near dusk, feeling positive that his squatters were not there, the little Indian stepped out of his foliage hideaway. He tiptoed to the cabin and edged down the side wall, listening for any sign of movement or noise. In the front of the log dwelling there was a wooden chair and an overturned washtub sitting on the porch. Manatoa peeked in the small window, expecting to see the fuzzy-haired woman or her white-haired brother. Thanks to his incredible good luck, there was no one home. He pulled the latch on the door and it opened with a loud creaking sound, making his heart thump loudly in his chest. He stepped into the room slowly and gingerly, looking about with large eyes. He was familiar with some of the white man's things from the time he spent at the school house in Alabama Ferry. He'd made a friend of a young school teacher. He'd been so fascinated with the world outside his nation and he paid frequent visits to the ferry town. That was when he started thieving for fun. He had been hiding in a hackberry tree, unnoticed as she was teaching the students. The school teacher waited to call attention to him after she'd dismissed the students, he remembered.

He was interested in finding some of those sweet fruits in a jar- that was good on anything. His tummy ruled when he went on scavenging missions. Maybe there would be some bread also. He looked under the beds, and at the items on the little shelf. He could not understand the pictures or all of lettering on the items, even though he wanted to. Manatoa was quite careful not to make a mess, as he didn't want the people to know he'd been about. They sure didn't have much- why, he had more in his wigwam that he'd picked up here and there in his adventures. He sat in the rocking chair and rocked rather violently back and forth to enjoy its function. The dutch oven, sitting covered over the fireplace, caught his eye. He jumped up, leaving the chair still rocking, to go and see what was in it.

"Pfftt." It was empty! Turning around to continue his raid, Manatoa took off the red bandana and laid it on the table. He picked up Sadie's green floral print bonnet and put it on his head, tying the strings as he continued to walk around. He picked up Sadie's hand mirror and looked it over. He was startled when he caught his reflection; he had never seen his brown face and black hair, so clearly. The silly green thing on his head had him laughing again. He couldn't believe they wore those on their head!

He stepped backward into the rocking chair as it slowed in its swaying, then he froze in mid stride. What was that noise? Manatoa thought to himself. Was he hearing the rattling and jangling, of a wagon? In a flash he slipped the jam, the bread loaf, and the mirror that was on the table into his bag with the squirrel and piece of antler. He pulled off the bonnet and laid it back on the table, then snagged the bandana and eased out the front door and across the yard to the tree line, he disappeared into the trees camouflaged by under green canopy of cover.

Maybe he'd wait a bit before heading back to his wigwam. He was sure there was more fun to be had. He couldn't have planned his evening better. He watched the dusk evening unfold. He couldn't make out all the brother and sister were saying, however, he felt sure that the crazy man and his horse were finally leaving. With him out of the way he could have great fun with the fuzzy-haired lady and white hair. He was waiting for his delightful opportunity. He sat cross legged on the ground and opened his sack to snack on the bread. However, his fuzzy tailed prisoner had helped himself and left the snack in crumbles. His stomach was going to give him away; it was so noisy. His bread was over half gone, but he needed the crazy man to be well out of range. He didn't need him returning to be a hero. So, he sat and munched on his leftover crumbled piece of bread to biding his time.

Chapter 23

After some time had passed, Manatoa snuck back up to the porch, squatting below the window being careful to not be seen or heard. There was much conversation going on inside. No matter to him; there were schemes to unravel. He had managed his patience and deliberately waited for the precise moment of action. The ranger was well away and no threat to him now. The two had been in the small log dwelling for a while. He carefully pulled out the piece of broken antler from the bag and put it up to the window. With the intent to strike fear in their minds, he began to pull the piece downward toward him, scratching of the window. It made such a piercing noise it hurt even Manatoa's ears. As painful as it was he endured it, listening intently to the sounds inside and preparing for the excitement to come. Moments like this is what he lived for! Pausing his cacophonous medley, he noted that it went completely silent in the cabin. He leaned forward, tucking his head down further, cupping his hand over his mouth to contain his laughing.

He reached up scratched the window again, and this time he paired the screeching noise with the growling imitation of a ferocious animal. The quiet inside turned to fumbling panic- now was the precise moment. He inched over to the door and grabbed the latch with one hand while the other hand was in the bag holding the tail of a very frightened and confused squirrel. He pulled up on the latch and gravity caught the door opening it but a crack. That was all the space he would need! He tossed the wound-up squirrel in and darted off for the woods. Oh what fun! He wished he was high on a perch to see. There were dishes flying, the candle light went out and pots and pans sailing and hitting the floor. Screaming, fussing, even a few gunshots racked off in the air. The light disappeared as the door flung open wide. He caught a passing glimpse of the rodent racing away across the yard and up the nearest tree.

Manatoa threw himself over in the grass, rolling on the ground and laughing hysterically. What a trick! That was his best yet he thought boldly to himself. With his eyes shut tight and moisture forming he chuckled till his belly hurt. His rejoicing was cut short as he heard the eerie sound of a "click click" that stopped him dead in his roll on the ground. He slowly opened his watery eyes and tried to focus in and saw the white-haired man staring down at him with the double barreled shotgun. He seemed much bigger up close in person than he'd imagined, not much bigger than Manatoa himself if he were standing upright. The skinny white-haired man with a gun, now *that* he hadn't anticipated. Immediately his mind whirled with options as he scanned everything around them.

"Look here, Sadie, I know what happened to my shotgun and my bandanna. We have a little sticky-fingered Indian thief!" Ollie shouted over his shoulder towards the cabin without taking his eyes off the boy.

Sadie responded to her brother by running up to see. "Stay back, Sadie, he could be dangerous." Ollie warned.

Manatoa was inching his way up slowly, in sly movements. He was squatting now and nearly to his feet. All he would be need would be for the shooter to take one glance away, and he would run like the wind. The wind was always his companion, challenging him to go faster.

"Be still- don't move! I tell you." Ollie commanded him, taking notice that he had changed positions and seemingly had an agenda.

"Ollie, don't shoot him, he's just a boy." Sadie pleaded.

"Just a boy? I know, he tried to kill me with that stampede of wild longhorns and we lost Jed as a result." Manatoa smirked a half smile and raised one eyebrow.

Ollie tilted his head sideways with a question following, "Sadie, does he understand us? ---- He'll keep thieving from us if'n I don't end this." Needing her voice and support, Ollie looked back at his frazzled sister. When he turned back again, the boy was gone. He'd disappeared without a trace in an instant into the woods that he came from. Left lying on the ground was his bag of treasures spilled open with the shotgun that he'd taken from Ollie at the creek.

"He's just hungry, Ollie, look. He took jam and the bread that was in the cabin." Sadie said.

"Yeah, well how do you explain the stampede, my rifle, the squirrel, or even the missing chicken? What about this mirror- did he need that too? "Ollie reasoned with a spit of anger in his voice. "I'm going to go after him, and track him down. This all ends tonight."

"You'll do no such thing, Oliver Hartmann it's late, and you can't possibly track an Indian in the dark. We are tired and a lot has happened today. I, for one, have had plenty of excitement for this one day of my life. Save something for tomorrow to worry about. Let's go in and salvage the cabin- please." With that final declaration, Sadie turned and made her way for the cabin. He knew by the sound of her voice that she was spent. It would do her no good to have him lost at night in the woods. The young man stood there speechless, his clothes disheveled and energy spent. He stared blankly into the woods, knowing that the Indian boy would be back and was probably watching him that very second.

Sadie pulled the quilt divider to and wanted to melt into her bed. Her emotion had felt like the highs and lows of the mountains they crossed all in one day. The service had been wonderful, real food for the soul, the rain was a blessing to the ground, and the departure suddenly of her dear friend was incomprehensible. The squirrel and Indian boy had purged what emotion hung as a remnant in her mind. She slid off her work dress and into her nightgown, not even taking a second glance over at the burning candle. Sadie had no care for her brother in that moment, as she buried her face in the feather pillow. Two tears softly fell as she closed her eyes and prayed.

"Thank you God, for our safety this night and look after Mr. Ham as my heart breaks into pieces."

Chapter 24

Days turned into weeks and Sadie wasn't sure if this ache in her heart would ever mend. She couldn't get Ham's kiss out of her mind. It was her first real kiss ever, and it was not supposed to end that way. Even though her handsome ranger gave no indication that he would be back, her soul yearned for his return. She had always imagined her first kiss would be from her future husband and they'd live happily together. Sadie just knew, with some unspoken tugging in her heart, this wasn't the last she'd seen of him. It couldn't end this way!

Fall had ended and the rainy season of winter had set in with little mercy. Ollie had managed to get some seeds for her to plant some greens for the winter garden, and with all the rain, it was tending fairly well. The pair worked together daily on projects as the weather permitted. They had processed out the hog and made soap from the lard. During the breezy days of fall, the pair of them managed to get the pole barn up for Maude.

It wasn't finished, but it certainly had come a long way, serving as windbreak and rain refuge for the bovine.

Mornings and nights passed without event, keeping the routines going on for the two of them. Sadie had her hand work to keep her busy in the early evenings, and Ollie his whittling before they both fell into their beds. Life just didn't seem the same. It was solemn with a quietness somehow, reminiscent of when their Mama and Poppa passed on. Ham had not died- and yet her heart felt like it bore a gaping hole with a piece missing.

Since the revival meeting, Ollie had found every excuse he could go and visit the MacDougal farm. Many days he accepted the gracious invitation by Mrs. MacDougal to stay on for supper. He'd taken quite an eye to their daughter, Alison. Ollie worked for Kershy once a week and paid off the young horse in no time. They promptly named her, Joy, as it was a true joy and blessing to add her to the farm. Ollie worked out a deal to walk their cow, Maude, over in the spring and get her bred back by Kershy's prized Scottish highland bull. He brought the red haired bull all the way from Scotland, and was quite proud of him. Mrs. MacDougal poked a bit of fun and called Kershy's prized bull, "His Lordship", a pet name that caught on with the cowhands.

In all of Ollie's visits working around the ranch, Kershy had taken a real liking to him. Mrs. MacDougal had shared with Sadie on more than one occasion that Kershy was right impressed with the boy. He had also said that Ollie has real natural talent and a strong back when it came to woodworking, and with a little leadership, he'd make a fine woodsman.

Sadie went with Ollie occasionally to visit the MacDougal Ranch. Their home and ranch was always bustling with all kinds of hectic enthusiasm. The two-story log home was finely furnished with all parts of functional pieces. It was nestled among a grove of oaks in the northwest corner of their two hundred and forty acres. With Mrs. MacDougal and her three daughters bustling around the home, there was always something to be done, a critical catastrophe might happen at any given moment. There was an assortment of ranch hands tending to cattle & horses and a ranch cook, fondly known as "cookie", who fed the crew in the outdoor kitchen near the bunk house. Sadie would have loved to have sisters to share the work and the joys in life! Alison's younger sister Bess liked to sew dresses, and the youngest daughter, Meredith, was always outside in a tree, in the barn, or busy with some critter that she rescued. Aly was her mother's right hand in the kitchen. It was really comforting to have some neighbors to share with and talk to. Mrs. MacDougal always had the newest contraption, Sadie thought. Mr. MacDougal loved to flatter her with ornaments for her kitchen from the special catalog at the general store.

On this night, the evening settled in with a chill in the air, "Ollie, you want some more coffee?" Sadie stood up from the rocker, pulling the quilt over her shoulders and sauntering slowly to the fireplace. She tossed a fresh cut of wood in and grabbed the handle on the blackened coffee pot.

"Sure Sis, I need a warmup."

"I just can't help thinking of Ham and that there is something wrong! Did you and Ham have words, and was he angry? Maybe he misunderstood something? I just don't understand why he left so suddenly." Sadie looked at Ollie with sincere eyes as she was filling his cup. She knew there was nothing that either of them could do. She just kept praying that God would protect him, wherever he was. "Did he say why he was leaving?"

"We've been over this a hundred times, Sadie. He said, he had to get back to check in with Captain Hayes in Austin. I sure wish there was more to tell. I don't know what was going on in his head, but I got the feeling he wasn't wanting to leave."

"I know! I just feel like I'm missing something - if there was just something that I could do" she paused and peered out the fogged window pane, looking at nothing in particular.

"I could pen a letter to Captain Hayes to see if he's had any word surely he's made it to his post by now." Sadie made the suggestion and felt immediately encouraged. She didn't wait for Ollie to agree or share his thoughts. Going over to the chest at the foot of her bed she found her letter box. Inside were some sheets of paper and a wooden pencil, nested with a few mementos that she kept safe there. There was a pressed flower from her grandmother's funeral, and a piece of dried grass from where her Mama lay. There was a scrap of fabric from Joe Wilson's shirt, ripped in a tug- of- war match between her and Suzy Smith. She wasn't real sure why she'd kept that- maybe she'd been sweet on him before they left for Texas. He was now a distant memory, and it seemed quite silly to still have that momento. In a small drawstring pouch were a few random buttons, her mother's ear screws, and a simple wedding band. She neatly put all the things back in place on top of her Sunday dress and bonnet.

"If the weather holds clear another day or so, I'll saddle Joy up and ride over to Alabama Ferry to post the letter and get any supplies we might need. I'll also ask around about that Indian boy we've not seen hide nor hair of since he set the squirrel loose in the cabin," Ollie announced. Sadie snickered as she sat down at the table and moved the candle closer to see her paper.

As she stared at the paper, plotting just how to begin her inquiry, a smile crept across her face. It really was a harmless prank- not funny at the time. The more she thought about it now, it was quite silly, and there was no real harm done. But it would be a while before Ollie saw it that way. As easygoing as his nature was, his pride was wounded, and he didn't like not knowing what the Indian was up to. She dipped her quill in the ink and began to form her strokes. If she were at liberty to pour out her heart she would write all her feelings and declarations of love onto the paper. Instead of standing awkwardly with total lack of literary talent, she could simply pen her love with deep frankness and care. It was not her beloved that she would be writing to- those declarations would have to wait. Exhaling a deep sigh, she began. "Dear Captain Hayes, . . ."

"Protect him Lord, God speed this letter, and let it find him in your favor."

Chapter 25

Opening his eyes, Ham felt around for his gun. Where was it? For that matter where was he? The last thing he remembered was the Navasota River, surrendering his heart to God, and being overwhelmed with the weight of his world being lifted from his shoulders. Unspeakable joy filled his soul as he recalled the experience smiling deep within his soul. He remembered nothing other than the feeling of warmth.

The room about him was dark, and everything around him was blurry and distorted. He struggled to make anything out. It looked like a cabin- could he really be back in Sadie's cabin? He tried to sit up, leaning forward and putting weight on his elbows as he struggled to support his body. His flesh was so weak; he had no energy or strength. Also, he couldn't think clearly; he was thirsty. He felt dry and parched like a desert. He could drink up that whole river if he could just get to it!

"Water?!" he said, with a dry raspy mouth. His tongue felt like cotton and his throat a blistered rub board. And yes, he was so cold, his toes felt like they were covered in a bank of snow.

"Shh… it's *all* right, you're safe- no need to be getting up just yet," the young voice reassured him. She leaned over the bed and wiped his brow with a cool rag. She held a dish to his lips and cradled his head to assist him in taking a sup of water. His mind was playing tricks on him. That chestnut hair he knew anywhere. And that voice was unmistakable. Those eyes, the most enchanting emerald eyes he'd seen anywhere. But how could that be? His headached and whirled with confusion.

"Sadie girl? I'm so sorry- forgive me for leaving like I did, I'm never leaving you again. You are the gravy on my corn cake- please stay at my fire."

"Shhh… rest now- save your energy," the calm soothing voice reassured him again. She reached to pat him gently on the chest to calm him. He took her hand within his and smiled as he lay back onto the pillow and was again enveloped by the deep heavy sleep.

"Do you reckon he's gonna make it, Pa?" The young girl said in a hushed whisper, while slowly sliding her hand away from his grip.

"I do. He's young, strong, and seemingly good health, I think he'll be just fine if'n that fever breaks soon. It's pretty high – he's seeing things that aren't so. He's had it on now a few days and who knows how longs he'd been there on that bank before we found him. From the looks of him and his scars he's had some near scrapes before- there's no doubt he's a fighter."

"Who do you think Sadie is, Pa?"

"I don't reckon I know-. She could be anyone in the territory."

"She must be special to this fellow." She said, tilting her head sideways and smiling softly.

"She?" he glanced up, wrinkling his forehead.

"Sadie.

"Likely so-, stoke that fire Nellie and go gather some beautyberry leaves that we can make a tea from to help bring down the fever, also heat some broth. We'll see if he'll take some in a bit. I'll go out and see to his horse and fetch some more hay. That horse was rode down pretty hard- I don't know what he was running from. If he doesn't come around soon, I'll ride over to the Fort Boggy and see if they know him. That ranger badge on his shirt says he's someone that'll be missed. You mind your chores, girl, and let the man be."

"Yes, sir," Nellie covered Ham up with the quilt and tucked him in warmly. She whispered, "I can't wait to be someone's Sadie."

Chapter 26

Manatoa had kept to himself since his episode with the white haired man and the shotgun. He did not for one second expect that reaction. Frankly he didn't believe the skinny white hair had it in him. It was funny, real funny right up to that moment when he was staring up the barrel of that gun. When the skinny man turned back to look at the fuzzy haired maiden, Manatoa shrewdly slinked away. The worst part was he lost all of his treasures. He'd played hard, and lost it all, to walk home empty handed.

He used to have a friend, a Tejano teacher that was teaching him to make English words. That had not ended well. He had enjoyed learning new things, but he could not go back there either. He'd not ventured to close to any villages or homesteads for days. His last episode would still be fresh on the man's mind and that was a good way to actually get shot- a particular outcome that Manatoa really wasn't interested in trying just yet.

The rain had filled up the river bed and the river was up now, making it difficult to sneak into the ferry towns on the opposite side of the river. He'd been keeping close to his wigwam and the warmth of his own fire. Aside from hunting small game for himself; he and his hungry belly kept out of sight. He stayed away from people to keep from getting caught. He'd been through all his treasures, made new arrows, and found nothing of interest. Boredom was beginning to wear thin and he was desperate for some distraction. Curiosity did have a hold on him; as did the need for adventure and suspense. He'd spent so much time watching the white - hair man he felt an odd connection to their family. He was not so friendly with them that he was free to tell tales that ended with a slap to the knee or a joke. Rather, he felt like he would be strangely sad if they were gone and his wood would be empty. Manatoa had no one. After what happened with the teacher, no one would ever accept him. He'd never felt more lonely than he did these days, as he'd been driven away from everyone and everywhere he went. He needed something to liven up his day. Maybe he'd walk over to the white - haired boy's place for a short visit- "I bet that fat cow needs to stretch her legs. Yes, a brilliant idea. What could that hurt?"

●

"I am very obliged to you, Senor Curador, and to you, young Miss Nellie, for taking such great care of me and my best pal Flip. Why, I think he's gained ten pounds loafing around being lazy these few weeks."

"It was my pleasure, amigo. If you are ever in need, stop in for a rest or just a visit you are most welcome here."

"Aw, are you sure you have to go? I bet your rush has something to do with that Sadie girl, doesn't it?" Nellie made the bouncy remark with her bubbling smile. She did have a small schoolgirl crush on Ham and hated to see him ride off for any girl.

"Nellie, mind your tongue!" Her father gave her a frowning look. Nellie, his late- in- life blessing, kept him young in spirit and gray in the roots. With no female presence in her life she had visions of her own, Spanish romance and family aspirations filling her unbridled thoughts.

"It's all right Senor. I am afraid Miss Nellie is right. I am overdue and have need to be elsewhere. I'll always be thankful for what you did." Ham said, while smoothing his hair back and settling his worn hat on his head.

"Here are some *frijoles con tortillas* for your journey."

"*Gracias*, much appreciated! God has given me a second chance and I intend to make the most of it."

"Safe travels *mi amigo*." Senor. Curador reached out to shake Hams hand one last time.

Ham turned and waved back at Senor Curador and Nellie. As they watched him ride away from their small homestead, they couldn't help but wonder if they'd ever see him again.

Ham's mind had never been so clear. He knew with no doubt what he wanted and where she was. There were just a few things that needed to be set straight first. If he hadn't been gone too long maybe he still had a job as a ranger. If not, well, he'd explore the idea of ranching. He had to hope that Sadie would still be waiting for him when he returned. He'd given her no such hope or promise, so she was well within her right to move on. He hoped like everything that hadn't happened yet. He kicked Flip into a trot- it was time to put some ground underneath them!

Chapter 27

January 1846

Ollie had made exceptional time as he traveled on Joy. She wasn't as frisky as Flip, but she got the job done. The Trinity had swelled its banks making a massive river crossing. Ollie hadn't felt this nervous about crossing the river since they came to this country. When they arrived then, the water was up, and they crossed with the wagon and all the animals on the ferry; unlike today, the river was bone-chilling cold. Ollie had no desire to get wet if he didn't have to. He held Joy's reigns and talked softly to her, really trying to reassure himself. The water was swift, brown, and cold lapping up on the edges of the raft. This was his least favorite part of the trip, yet a necessary one to make it.

Alabama Ferry was a bustling and busy frontier town, at least this time of year. The river's being up meant steamships arriving regularly from the South. Hanson's Store would have a vast assortment of supplies and goods. Ollie set out to post Sadie's letter first, next he'd check in at the general store and see if he could swap some pelts for salt, chicory, sugar, and a few yards of pretty fabric for Sadie. She needed the cheering up, and she'd love to have a new frock even if she wouldn't admit it.

Sadie had packed him a lunch so he wouldn't have to stop in at the café. After his last experience there and the great purge afterward, he wasn't too keen on visiting again. This time, he'd keep an eye out for those trouble-making Hanson boys. Mr. Hanson seemed like a fair man in all his dealings until his boys were concerned. Then fairness gave way to a gruff exterior and he didn't seem to want to be bothered with their boyish shenanigans. When Ollie mentioned his previous mishaps Hanson chalked it up to, "well you know boys." and promptly turned with increased busyness.

When Ollie had made his rounds at the usual stops each time he inquired about the Indian boy, but no one had anything to share; they hadn't seen anyone by that description. Ollie did meet a fellow with hens for sale. He traded the man his pocket watch that didn't tick anymore. A fair trade he thought, and Sadie would have six new hens to add to her brood. He had hopes that the family would be growing soon, and they'd need more than just two eggs a day. He looped the rope on the burlap bags containing the birds over the saddle horn.

Ollie was *determined* to find out something on that Indian boy. So far no one had any information, or they wouldn't give any. Everywhere he went they were talkative, right up until he asked about Indians, from Hanson's General Store on to Jim the farrier! Ollie walked the length of Main Street, following it to the end. He got to the end of the town trail he found the remains of a building that had burnt to the ground. It had been a total loss; only a few half-burned boards lay around. Next to the burned remains was a scorched hackberry tree. Half of it was blackened and the other barren from the loss of foliage from the winter months. Beneath it was a wooden cross, with a pink satin ribbon tied in a bow.

Ollie led Joy to the hitching post and wrapped the rein in a slip knot. He hadn't noticed the building before on his previous trip. He'd been so excited about riding Flip, with all the emotion bearing down, he hadn't really taken in the sights of the little settlement. Had it been burnt for a while? He walked in the burned traces of the building looking about, not expecting to find anything.

"Right sad- isn't it?" an old fellow appeared from nowhere, it seemed to Ollie, he was staggering about, obviously inebriated. His jacket was tattered and frayed, and his hair was uncut; also, he smelled of old liquor and onions.

"What's that?" Ollie questioned.

"This here schoolhouse burned down with the eldest Isaac's daughter, the young school marm, inside."

"You don't say!" Well, now he was really curious and had to hear this story. He walked closer to the disheveled man.

"I do say! I might have seen the whole thing. If you have two bits, I'll tell you more." The slurring raggedy old fellow wobbled over to the tree and leaned against it for support. Feeling like he was fixing to "get took," Ollie reached into his vest pocket and handed the old timer two bits anyway.

"Well, I said two for information-"he suggested, wanting more.

"You have that. Now tell the story," Ollie declared. He didn't cut the red rascal any slack; his face was turning red with impatience.

"That there Injun boy done it, I saw it with my own eyes!"

"Indian boy? What boy? What did he look like?" He was now knee deep engrossed and couldn't get answers fast enough. He walked over even closer to the man so he could hear every slurring syllable. The whiff of onion was just nearly too much as he checked himself and stepped back a half step while wincing his eyes.

"He looked like an Injun! What do you think he looked like! He wanted to learn to speak English and to read. You can't teach them to read. The school marm, that young gal, she was innocent, I tell ya. She argued with him and he set the building on fire. I know he attacked her and burned the building down. She must have been in a bad way to not get out of there."

"Why, what do you mean she didn't get out of there? If you saw the whole thing, why didn't you help? What happened?" Ollie pestered, impatient for answers.

"That's all I know. It happened too fast, and you best be going on your way too. Folks don't take kindly to strangers asking so many questions." The old timer stumbled away across the street, fumbling for his flask, and mumbling incoherently to himself.

"You can't start a story and leave it like that!" Ollie yelled across the dirt street at the man. The old fellow slumped over and he slunk away, pretending to be deaf.

There were so many more questions, and things that just didn't make sense, but one thing was for sure. That Indian boy was trouble. And if he saw him around his homestead, he wouldn't wait to ask questions. "I've got to get home and tell Sadie- she could be in real danger."

"Lord protect Sadie and give Joy a swift trot."

Chapter 28

Sadie had just sent the letter with Ollie to be posted; she knew there was no way he'd have word back this soon, but she wished that were the case. At least it wasn't raining but it was frigidly cold. Sadie slipped her slim feet, layered with socks, into her Poppa's old boots, pulling the bonnet on her head and tying it securely. She grabbed her shawl and wrapped it around her shoulders over the sweater she was already wearing. She put on her gloves and thrust open the cabin door. Walking out, she was quickly reminded of the brisk wind, bitter and nasty. "However, the chores don't tend themselves," she thought as she walked away leaving the cabin door open. Mama had always told her that in the winter if they wanted to keep sickness away- she'd need to cool down the cabin, let the fire die, and let the house get bone cold.

Keeping busy, she made her rounds, collecting eggs and feeding all the critters. Maude had been cooped up for days in her little makeshift stall. Sadie and Ollie had built it together to get her out of the rain, and Kershy had come to help with the logs for the roof. It was a basic log shed with an open side that faced the south to block the north wind. She needed to get the chilled jersey out and stretch her legs. Sadie looped the rope to make a halter, catching the cow's nose and head. She secured it on her and gave Maude a tug. "Come now, Maude, some fresh air and movement will do us both some good." The cow let out a defiant moo and ambled out of the stall against her better judgement.

Sadie walked her about the property, around the cabin, the outhouse, smokehouse, chicken shack, and past the small garden. Maude got an eye full of cabbage and spinach greens in the rectangular patch and it was all Sadie could do to keep her focused on the path.

Returning Maude to her stall, Sadie rubbed her and fed her a handful of corn kernels. She grabbed an arm - load of firewood to take in the cabin, and then she saw the empty water pail. She'd have to go all the way down to the creek to fetch water! She dropped the small stack of wood in the cabin by the cold hearth and emptied her apron pockets of the eggs. Leaning up against the doorjamb sat Poppa's shotgun. She didn't need it, as she'd be right back: it was far too cold to dawdle. Grabbing just the bucket on her way out the open door, Sadie headed down to the creek.

The little stream wasn't so far from the cabin, but the trek down was somewhat a challenge in inclement weather; it was down a steep hill that was no fun when rainy. Occasionally, they had flooding, and Poppa didn't want the cabin anywhere near that overflow. "God's creation even in the winter months is quite beautiful," Sadie thought to herself. The pine and cedar trees still carry their green and stand out like green beacons of hope in the grey brown landscape, even if the oaks, gums, and hackberries had lost all their beautiful colored leaves. These leaves provided a moist, carpet to walk upon. She walked carefully, watching where she placed her feet, as she trudged with the oversize boots on. This time of season was miserable for people and animals. The creek was swollen and flowing briskly. It would be *so* cold to get wet and also dangerous! She was thankful she didn't have to. Dipping her bucket into the stream, she collected some water.

Taking in the view Sadie looked about wondering and hoping Ollie would be home before too long. Pulling the shawl tight around her shoulders and warming her hands with her breath, she wondered where Ham was. Was he somewhere warm, or stuck out on a wet, cold trail? She couldn't help but wonder if he was okay. Full bucket. . .back up this hill she had to go. It was a steep incline with a sandy slope that turned to slippery mud when wet. She picked up the hem of her skirts with one hand, the water pail with the other, and began the trudge up the hill. Stopping half way and taking a breath something caught her glance in her peripheral vision. She looked up in the oak tree with its branches extending over and out. On the long horizontal branch lay a massive cougar. Sadie's face paled and fear washed over her. The large cat opened his mouth, yet she heard nothing come out. She took it as a threat and wondered what to do. To continue forward would mean walking underneath the branch that this lion inhabited. Where was her rifle? She hadn't brought it. How could she have been so careless? What was she thinking?

She'd been thinking about Ham, that's what! And look where it got her. Oh how she wished he were here, or Ollie- or Poppa, for that matter. *They'd* know what to do. She took a half step backwards without moving her face and her eyes set on this feline and watching his every move. The cougar began to rise from his half- lazy stance. He'd made her acquaintance and wasn't content to let her walk away. She gently bent her knees and set the water pail down on the hill side. She just wasn't sure what to do. She could run for the cabin, but she was half way up the hill. She'd never make it, not in these cumbersome shoes! She could run towards the creek and hope he didn't want to go for a swim. That wasn't appealing either. Either way- she felt doomed to disaster.

The creek was water her best and only option. Sadie took two more quick steps backward, while the cougar perched on all fours, ready to leap at any moment. His warning was being heard clearly as his snarling threat echoed off of the creek bank. Sadie turned quickly, picking up her skirts and running for her life. In her flight, her shawl came off and fell to the ground. She tripped and fell over her own feet in eagerness to get away. The cougar leapt from the tree and fell flat on the ground with an unmistakable thud. She looked back in haste to see the animal lying there with an arrow through his chest. She turned to see where the arrow came from and there stood the little Indian boy. He'd just saved her life! He turned to walk away "Hey, don't go please…WAIT-" Sadie called urgently.

"Please, don't go. I wish to thank you. My name is Sadie. Do you understand?" Sadie stood, covered in sand and mud.

"Yes- I can make your words." The boy replied.

"Wonderful!" Still reeling from the death of the cougar, she pressed for more conversation. "How did you learn English?"

"The teacher in the ferry town across the great river- she teach me. You tell them I not hurt her!" Manatoa slung his bow over his back. He walked past Sadie to the dead cougar lying on the path to the cabin, pulling his arrow from the beast's chest. He stuck his finger in the wound to get the warm blood, then he made a swipe across his forehead and down his nose.

"Wait, - I don't understand. Tell who?" Sadie asked. As she walked toward him. He was a small boy, not looking any older than twelve but he had mature look to his face. His hair was long, stiff, and black, with a white feather that blew in the brisk wind; he had a stern brow and a proud nose.

"Stop there!" Ollie had pulled the long barreled shotgun from its scabbard. Standing stiff in the stirrups with a slight tremble in his elbows he had the long-barreled gun sighted straight for Manatoa.

"Ollie, stop! You don't understand!" Sadie warned him. Ollie pulled back the hammer and didn't move a muscle. Sadie walked towards Ollie with her hands in the air.

"I understand completely, Sadie, he killed a woman in town, and I won't let him kill you."

"What are you talking about Ollie?" Sadie pleaded. "He just saved my life."

Ollie paused in his stance and glanced over at Sadie. He was quite confused. He sat back down in the saddle, still pointing the rifle in the Indian's direction. Manatoa slid the arrow back into his quiver, wiping his hand on his hide pants. He picked up the cougar and slung him over his shoulders, walking silently into the thicket and disappearing.

"Thank You Lord," she sighed quietly.

Chapter 29

"I should not have let him go like that!" Ollie was still angry. "We should have demanded answers. A woman was killed in town, and they believe he did it."

"I don't! Ollie- he's had more than one opportunity to kill us. I think he would have taken that chance already. I think he's lonely. Poppa said the tribes in this area just packed up and left with no word long before we came. What if somehow he got left behind?"

"Sadie, you didn't see that school house. There was nothing left but a pile of ash."

"You are right, but he didn't have to save me from that cougar." Sadie argued.. Ollie couldn't deny that, and yet he wasn't sure how to make sense of the whole situation.

Once inside the cabin, Sadie got up and lit the candle on the table with an ember from the hearth and began setting the table for their evening meal. Ollie stood up from his rocking chair and paced around the room.

Sadie hadn't noticed that her brother seemed two inches taller just recently. He'd filled out in his shoulders, looking not half as scrawny.

"What else is on your mind, Ollie? Did you post the letter? Have you had word from Ham?"

"Yes, I posted the letter, and no, I haven't heard anything. I need to ask you something, Sadie, and you have to be honest with me."

"Sure thing, Ollie, you know I will," his sister replied. But what is this about? Did something happen in town?"

"I want to ask Alison MacDougal to marry me."

"Really, that's fantastic! I was wondering when you were going to get your courage up." She was smiling while fetching plates to set the table.

"Do you think that I have a chance?" Ollie asked nervously, biting his lip.

"A chance? That girl would be plum silly not to say yes. And she will say yes, she's crazy about you. Oh, Ollie, congratulations! – I am so excited for you and me too-I get a sister!"

"Well, I haven't asked her yet. - I have to talk to Mr. MacDougal and get his permission first. What if he says no?" Ollie wiped his hands on his pants legs and paced around the room.

"Don't even think about it, Oliver. Where would ya'll live?" Sadie inquired.

"Well, here! I can't *imagine* living anywhere else. I wouldn't be putting *you* out, Sadie. I'd never do that. I'd thought I might close in the leanto for you. It's partially completed and it would make a right cozy room that would be real private-like for you."

"That would be splendid," Sadie said, aloud while on the inside she felt a twinge of disappointment. It really wasn't sadness for Ollie or the leanto; she wanted him to be happy. She really liked Alison, and she knew the young girl was a very competent cook and keeper of the house. She and Ollie would make a striking pair. She was just a hair taller than Ollie when he slumped! However, she wouldn't mention that just now! She had beautiful creamy white skin, her lovely red hair! No, the disappointment was for her and her beau, who never was really her beau. She had no word, promise, or guarantee, just this nagging feeling that he *might* be back. The longer the days dragged on, even that hope began to dwindle away.

"Well, that settles it," Ollie declared. "I'm going to talk to her Pa- directly. I'd like to ride over tomorrow. Would you like to go with me? You could visit with the MacDougal ladies."

●

His whole reunion had gone better than Ham had anticipated. General Hayes had been relieved that he'd not lost one of his best rangers. With his orders in hand, Ham headed the way he wanted now, straight for deep East Texas. There was no way he could beat that letter the General sent back to Sadie. She would be crushed when she got it. The best he could do would be try to get back there as soon as he could. All those trials aside, Ham knew that God had truly shown his favor over him. He could see it so clearly now. God had spared him each time, protecting him from certain death and disease. All the moments in his life he thought had been curses from God were the hand of God moving him and directing him to a time in his life he'd waited all his years for.

Ham pushed onward into the east wind, driven with more determination and purpose than he'd felt in all his years. *"God! Protect her"* he prayed aloud. He didn't have to say her name. God knew just the one Ham was petitioning for. He rode steady crossing the plains, using every minute the sun would spare, and even borrowed some time from the moon.

The thought of a hot meal, corral for his old pal Flip, and a warm bed to share was most desirable. Those defining dimples, slight curvature of the waist, and those small farmgirl hands belonged to the woman he needed. Her silly sweet innocence, walking adventures, and sick days-he wanted them all. The only thing that separated them was the vast space of Texas. Home never sounded so good. Would she even have him? He didn't exactly leave her with as much as a hint of his return.

Flip skipped a step, awakening Ham from his daydream. "Whoa, boy!" Pulling up on the reins and easing his grip, Ham saw there was a problem. The horse had a notable gimp in his step. The ranger stepped out of the saddle and patted Flip to ease his nerves. Pushing Flip in the chest, and he gave a click or two for him to step backwards. Sure enough, it was the front right hoof. Bending his leg up for a look, Ham detected a rock impressed in the hoof. He used his knife to pick it out and clean the area but, the damage was done. Flip had a nasty stone bruise that wouldn't heal if he continued riding. He'd have to rest for a few days. He took in his surroundings, deliberating his options. If he wasn't mistaken, over the next rise was the homestead of his friend Senor Curador with his homestead close to the river. He slowly led his limping friend to their refuge.

Nellie saw Ham coming and ran to get her father. The old man was silver-headed and walked with a crippled leg, but that didn't seem to slow him down. He came out limping, weaving, and just a-wobbling back and forth with excitement to greet his guest.

"Buenos Dias, my ranger friend! I did not expect to see you so soon."

"Hello Senor." Ham grinned with relief to see his wise friend. They exchanged embraces and remarked on how well the other looked.

"Is there something that I can help you with, Senor Ranger?"

"Do you have space for Flip to rest up for a while?"

"Si, this is God's providence." Senor Curador said, as he reached to grab Flips reins and the pair limped to the barn. "Come my friend, we shall find you a treat for your labors."

Nellie, with all of Ham's attentions, had a hundred questions about *everything*. He adored her, he just couldn't help it! He'd wished he'd had a little sister to dote upon. He reached into the saddle bags and presented her with a stick of licorice, and her smile was warming to his soul.

Coffee, a warm taco, and great conversation were the marks of a quality visit with Senor Curador on his homestead. Ham's host had much wisdom and many stories to share from his life experience. However, Ham would have to postpone those stories for a later visit. He was on a mission with fervency that couldn't be harnessed. Senor Curador recognized this and knew he could not be swayed. He quickly led out his bay mare to be saddled.

Ham, in one firm motion, put his saddle on the bay mare. Flip nickered and stomped in protest, pawing at the ground. This was eating both of them up! He hated to leave him behind but the horse needed rest and he had no time to spare. They were an odd pair- but they were brothers bonded together by time, grief, and loss.

Talking aloud, he tried his hardest to justify his plan to his oldest companion. "I have to do this, but I'll be back for you, I promise. Old man, you eat up and rest well, and be ready to ride when I get back. That's an order – not a request." "His rock and hard place" had never felt so hard, yet he knew what he must do.

Nellie popped up from round behind the wagon. "I'll take good care of him, Senor Ham."

"I'm counting on it. He's right special to me." The ranger slung his leg over the bay mare and spun her on her heels to ride out quickly. He didn't look back, for fear they would see the tears in his eyes.

Chapter 30

"Kershy, what brings you out our way?" Ollie asked, very surprised to see his neighbor.

"I'm on me way back from Alabama Ferry and thought I'd drop ye post."

Sadie stood looking on nervous anticipation. All she'd heard was he had their post. She quickly finished the apple cobbler she was making, trying to remember to be lady-like and follow protocol. Kershy stepped down off his sorrel roan and looped the rein on the post. Ollie cleared his throat, "we are obliged to you for the trouble. Come on in and have seat." Ollie slid the letter into his pocket and motioned for Sadie to put the kettle on, but she didn't want to make tea or small talk; she wanted to read that letter!

"I needed to talk to you, Sir, on an important matter." Ollie began.

She just couldn't interrupt Ollie. "Oh dear," she thought to herself "He's doing *this* now". I suppose he has more pressing matters on his mind than finding out what that letter says. However, it was all she could do to keep her cool.

"I was just about to pay you Joy and saddle up a visit with you, Sir." Ollie was now turning red- faced and feeling so horribly embarrassed that he was tongue-tied. "Forgive me, Sir. What I meant to say was, I was going to saddle up Joy and come for a visit at your ranch with-

Kershy saved him from going on with an interruption to his thought. "You were? What have you need of, Son? Is the old heifer doing all right?" Kershy asked.

"Yes sir, Maude is just fine," Ollie answered, feeling a little calmer.

Sadie handed each of them a warm cup of coffee and let herself out the cabin door. She would bake her birthday treat later. Ollie was nervous, but he didn't need her help. She'd grabbed her gloves and shawl by the door, thinking she needed a walk and fresh air to calm her soul and spirit.

"Lord, whatever the letter says, grant me the peace to accept the contents and your will."

She'd replayed that day Ham went to the service with her over and over in her memory. She could kick herself in the fanny for not listening more closely or doing more for him while he was there. *"God, I don't want to lose him."* The warm tears came flowing down her chilled cheeks, although she didn't think that she had any left to spare. She sure wished her Mama was there to comfort her and help her make sense of things. She walked about and sat down on the ground on top of the cliff on one side of the property. The sand had washed out below, making for a sudden drop towards the creek bottom. It was her favorite spot; she wanted to have Ollie build a bench to put just here. The view was always enthralling. The leaf canopy had fallen now and Sadie could see the otherwise hidden creek bottom for miles across. Poppa would have loved this view. She pulled her handkerchief out of her sleeve, and was wiping her red tearful eyes when Ollie approached.

Without saying a word, he handed her the letter and turned to walk back to the cabin. She almost didn't want to open the letter and read the contents, knowing that the facts inside meant she must accept whatever the truth was and move on with her life. As much as she wanted this closure, she wasn't ready to let go of her love. She broke the seal and unfolded the crisp paper. The letter had gotten damp and the ink was smudged but still legible.

January 23, 1846

Dear Miss Hartmann,

It is with deepest regret that I reply with earnest haste. Mr. Hamlet Abner, Texas Ranger, that you wrote inquiring of has failed to report and therefore has been listed as missing. In my years' experience I have known him to be a most dedicated soldier and Texan. He has no other living relatives. I fear the worst has overtaken him. Please accept my sincerest condolences.

Captain Coffee Hayes, Texas Rangers

She buried her head and the tears erupted again. *"Here I am Lord, on my twentieth birthday! This is too much, Lord, and I cannot bear this."*

Softly within her spirit she heard, *"My grace is sufficient for thee- even you, Sadie."* She paused her emotion, knowing the Lord had not forgotten her. As she stared into bare trees, clutching the letter as her final link to her love, she dabbed the tears from her eyes. Broken in spirit, feeling alone, and pleading with God, she searched for strength.

A lovely redbird lighted on the limb of the oak tree extending above her head. The redbird stood out so boldly with its brilliant color, twitching it's movements against the browns and grays of the world of winter before her. She watched his manner and remembered that the Lord promised to take care of her just as he clothes and feeds the birds.

What an amazing promise. She felt a breath of peace, sadness still in her heart- but a sweet breath of peace. The bird flew and her attention was directed away to the right. There stood the little Indian boy.

"God please grant me grace."

•

"Hello there, would you like to talk?" She spoke calmly without moving a muscle, showing no fear or worry.

"Yes- I speak to you and tell you Manatoa's story." He spoke clearly, and remarkably well. She shifted in her seating, facing towards him. Taking a deep breath and folding her hanky she cleared her throat.

"Manatoa? Is that you?" Sadie questioned, drying the last of the moisture from her face.

"Yes- me- I tell you story- you listen."

"Ok, Sadie said. "Should I go get Ollie-my brother? Does he need to hear this?"

"No, white hair is no good for talkie- what do they call you?"

Sadie frowned, but afterward thought maybe he was trying to be funny. She wrapped her shawl around her tightly and stared at him with undivided attention.

"You can call me Sadie. It is very nice to meet you, Manuhh. How do you say your name again?"

"Listen – Man Uh toe ah. Now you say, Manuhhtoeah."

"Maneouhtoeahha." She scrunched her nose, knowing she hadn't got it right.

He sat down cross legged across from her as so they could hear each other easily. "I go to school house to learn white man's words. My mother was from Mexico and my father was an Indian brave. They are no more. I know not their stories. I sneak to village to play tricks. I hide in the tree to hear teacher teach the village children. She see me and talk to me. She not hit me or kick. She kind to me and feed me bread with jam. She ask me to come to school house with other children. My Kickapoo grandmother says, NO- no good." Bowing his head he speaks softly, "I not listen to her and I go. Village teacher teach me to talk and understand words."

"What happened next?" Sadie urged him sympathetically.

"All kids gone and I want to learn more words." He paused as though he were searching for the words. "I know not what happen. There was big boom of fire, smoke, and heat. The boom threw me into the teacher; I had hot fire on my back. She no fire, but blood everywhere. She would not move or wake up. I try to carry her but I could not, so. I ran away. I was scared and afraid of what they would think of me. I run just as fast as I can run to my village."

167

Manatoa showed little emotion; it was as though he was in a trance, reliving the story as he told it. Sadie was petrified and now crying again, but not for her sake. She believed every word of his tale, knowing he had nothing to gain by sharing his story with an outsider.

"When I came back out of breath and tired my Kickapoo Grandmother and whole tribe were gone. I not find them even to this day. I am the last of my people."

Sadie's face reflected anguish and grief for this young boy and his troubles. He is all alone with no one left in the world. She and Ollie had to help him in some way. However, she knew it would take some convincing to get Ollie on board! She felt at that very moment that she was blessed. She had a home with Ollie, with new friends and a sister-in- law to be.

"I am so sorry for your loss." She tried to reassure him but didn't know quite what to say.

"Would you like to come in for some bread and jam? It is my birthday and I would very much like your company." Sadie stood and led the way back to the cabin. He followed in at a distance.

"Lord, please let me help my new friend."

Chapter 31

Time was the enemy. With each passing day, Sadie just couldn't accept the fact that Ham was possibly gone forever. She tried to put him out of her mind as the cold winter days drew to a close. The ranch was looking for spring. Ollie and Alison would be getting married in April when the flowers were at their peak bloom. She'd have a sister to talk to and someone to share the woman work with. Ollie had the addition on the cabin fully enclosed and was sparing no effort for his sister. He'd built her bed on the far end with a small table for her wash bowl. The best feature of all that Sadie loved most about her new location was the wood floor.

Ollie's soon-to-be father-in-law opened a saw mill in Raymond, enabling Ollie to get some trees cut into lumber. The cabin didn't even have a wood floor but it wouldn't be long and that would be installed. There had been some talk about Ollie and Alison living over at the MacDougal Ranch. It was no secret that with no sons, Kershy had his hands full with his cows, the lumber mill, and the homestead. However, Ollie felt that it was his responsibility to make a go of the Hartmann homestead. This land was his father's heritage, the only thing he had left to give. His gave everything he had to get it, Ollie thought. That couldn't be overlooked so easily.

The wedding was to be at the MacDougal Ranch. Sadie had cooked, prepared food, sewed herself a new dress with bonnet, and made gifts for the couple. The blue print with little purple flowers that Ollie had picked made a becoming dress for the day. Sadie's green eyes were bright and enchanting against the blues and purples.

She wasn't sure she was ready for this day. She had felt like she'd come to terms with the fact that Ham wasn't coming back. However, she just wasn't ready to entertain questions from all the ladies at Raymond on the subject, nor was she looking forward to entertaining dance partners who were looking for a future wife.

She would pause when working in the garden if the wind blew a certain way, and look for that stoic face that she fell in love with. While working in the cabin, she'd heard the jingle of his silver dollar spurs on the porch. At night she dreamed of his warm embrace and safe arms around her. If her mind and heart would simply comply, she could move on.

Ollie was more nervous than that squirrel in the cabin. He fretted around making sure all the chores were over-tended and the cabin was just perfect for his new bride. Sadie had moved her things to the new addition and packed the last few remaining crates of food and supplies for the ride over to the MacDougal's.

"It's all going to be just fine, Ollie. Stop pacing around and help me load the wagon. I didn't cook for two days to leave it all behind." she said forcefully.

"Sadie, what if I forget my vows?"

"That's silly-you won't-"

"What if I drop the ring?"

"Then you pick it up." She declared, as she passed him the last crate and closed the cabin door.

"What if? . . ."

"No more what if's…. you'll do just fine." Sadie reassured him. He plopped down in the wagon seat next to her and grabbed the reins, and she reached up and smoothed his white hair, straightening his vest on his shoulders. Looking at her brother, she gasped with a deep breath, and her eyes filled easily with moisture. He looked five years older just since they arrived here. She couldn't possibly feel any more proud of him than she did at this very moment! Ollie returned the love in his sister's face with a kiss on her forehead.

"We can't keep Alison waiting…Get up!" Ollie clicked his tongue and slapped the reins on Joy. The realization of the day filled him with a nervous excitement he'd never known. This evening he would make his trip back home - with a bride sitting by his side! He'd give anything for his Poppa to be here.

"God, bless this day- I dedicate it to you, God."

•

Kershy had spared no expense for his eldest red-haired beauty. A large tent was erected, just as before the revival. The community of Raymond had begun construction on a church house, but it was still a shell of a building. There were long tables on one side of the tent, with quilts draped as table cloths. There was a collection of mismatched chairs and rockers and few rows of benches lined along one side of the tent.

Alison's younger sister had picked a basket full of black-eyed Susans, bachelor buttons, and Indian paint brushes. She'd placed the small bouquets in little crocks lining the center of the tables everything was beautiful and fresh. The God-given décor was lush green grass from the rainy winter and green trees budded out with colorful blooms. The scenery was simple and yet enchanting.

The whole town had come out for this occasion. It would to be the event of the year right after the area-wide revival. Ollie looked sharp in his new gray breeches and white shirt, with a matching grey vest and a smart new hat. Sadie scanned the area and found him standing nervous talking to Kershy and Wildcat Morrell. No doubt he was getting his orders and instructions on how the service would go.

"No, dearie, this goes down here." Sadie had been trying to assist Mrs. MacDougal in the organization of the food. Clearly she was used to being in charge; she moved everything Sadie arranged! Sadie was easily distracted, with her mind nowhere and everywhere at the same time. She found herself scanning the people looking for a familiar face, a particular face.

Young Bess McDougal stole Sadie away from the women for a half second. She had a large smile, and a mysterious flutter in her eyes. She leaned toward Sadie and whispered loudly, having trouble containing her exhilaration.

"Guess what? I'm in love! Sadie." She opened her hand and shown a small oblong emerald brooch.

"Where did you get that, Bess?"

"He gave it to me- aren't I so special?" Bess winced like a childish school girl, blushing. She closed her hand again to conceal her gift.

"Bess, seriously- who gave this to you? That is no trinket?" Sadie whispered, now pulling her further away from the voices under the tent.

"Cole Blackhert- he just started working for my Da. Have you seen him? He's so handsome, and he says he wants to marry me. He was a gunfighter out west and wants to see the world."

"Was or is a gunfighter? The real question is, what's he doing here then, Bess?" Sadie grabbed her hands and stared directly into her eyes.

"Well, I don't know Sadie- that doesn't matter much. Oh, don't tell Mum- she'll spoil the fun and promise me you won't tell my Da" Bess pulled away, seeing the concern misread as disapproval in Sadie's face.

"Bess, let's talk about this," Sadie tried to reason with her.

"I thought you'd understand! He's not going to leave me like that Ranger left you!" Before Sadie could get another word out, Bess had deserted her, leaving her feeling nervous and worried for her friend's situation. Sadie loved spontaneous gesture but this sounded reckless. If she couldn't talk some sense into Bess, she'd need to share this with her parents. That would be a most difficult way to start a new family relationship.

Chapter 32

Ham arrived at the Hartmann homestead about midday. He stepped down from the sweaty mare and lapped the rein over the post on the corral. He noticed a rope halter slung over the gate post and hoofprints. "Ollie must have gotten a horse- Good deal."

He looked around, but saw no one. At first glance he noticed the new addition on the cabin and couldn't help wonder as to its purpose. He unloaded the rider from the pouch in his leather saddle bag and set him on the ground. He checked the newly enclosed barn and found Maude peacefully chewing her cud. Captain Crockett seemed accounted for, as were the presence of a few more hens, so he decided not to stick his head in the coop. Feeling as if he'd missed something important, he went to the cabin, saving it for last. Ham rapped on the door, waiting for a response. Nothing. He peeked in the window to rule out anything amiss, then walked out from the porch and looked more closely at the tracks. As he suspected, he saw wagon tracks leading towards Raymond. That was his best bet.

Retrieving the lead rope he led the mare over into the corral for a drink of water, now that her breathing had slowed. He could go looking for them or he could wait here. He couldn't wait. He'd come this far, so why stop now? He'd covered a great deal of distance in these few days; minus Flip and his stone bruise, it had been a pretty smooth trek. He gathered up his stowaway and nestled him back in the bag, setting out for Raymond. He wasn't sure what he'd say or how he'd begin, but she deserved the truth.

●

The ceremony in the cool of the late afternoon was just divine; Ollie didn't forget his lines or drop the ring. The wedding party was just beginning after they had completed the service and were preparing to begin eating, but the shameful entry of a herd of goats marked beginning of the reception. The normally free-range critters had escaped their confinement and wandered into the tent filled with guests. Before the men could say "scat," the billy goat jumped up on the dessert table, taking a large bite out of the double layer carrot cake that sat perfectly in the middle of the table. He must not have liked the taste of it, as he curled his top lip and stuck out his tongue with a bellow. He jumped down just as a mob of men were about to pounce on him for ruining the reception table; the women followed with brooms and angry threats. Soon there was a scattering mob of goats on the run, knocking things over and blazing a trail.

Sadie was pretty sure she saw a nanny goat running away with a blue sash in its mouth- she couldn't help but wonder if that was for a little goat bonnet.

It had been good to get off of the homestead for the day. It had taken her mind off the lonesomeness that had all but dominated her thoughts. The dance was just beginning, and she'd been avoiding eye contact with a rough-looking cowpoke all evening. She felt his eyes on her all afternoon, and she'd not a desire to return the gesture. However, she felt sure he'd come asking for his turn to dance. Spotting Meredith sitting alone; Sadie sauntered over to make some quiet inquiries. Meredith wasn't interested in this whole dress-up wedding occasion; she thought the whole mess to be overdone and entirely too much fuss. She was sitting alone petting her newest kitten.

"Don't look now, but have you seen that greasy haired, burly face, cowboy in the red calico shirt over yonder?" Sadie inquired.

"The smelly gross old guy—yeah. His name is D. He is one of Da's new cowhands."

"I figured so, by the swagger in his walk and the grisly exterior he has going. He's been following me all afternoon with his eyes, and he makes my skin crawl!" Nothing about this man was inviting. Sadie had not even met him, and she already had a bad feeling about him.

"He stinks so bad my horse Blue baby smells better than he does. I'll introduce you to him if you are interested." Meredith said with sarcasm.

"I think I'll pass on this one."

The string band began tuning up and scratching out a tune. Sadie excused herself and went to find a group of ladies to shuffle into and pretend to be interested in their conversation. She joined in passing conversations of quilts, pies, and the best remedy for bugs in the garden. Those were just the sort of distractions that she needed. If lucky, she'd be considered uninterested, and passed over for the first dance.

Ollie and his new bride took center of the tent and slow-danced a waltz. Mama and Poppa had not been much on dancing socials, but this was a special occasion. As the second dance was about to begin, Kershy stepped in and asked to dance with his baby girl, Alison. Being left unattended, Ollie came and grabbed Sadie's hand. "Would you dance with me, little sister?" Ollie bowed. She just couldn't turn him down!

"I would be so honored." She smiled sweetly. He escorted her to the center and danced a waltz with her that Ma would have been proud of. "I'm so happy for you, Ollie, and very proud to be your sister," she whispered.

"Proud of me? For what?"

"You are being modest. You have worked so hard on the homestead to do everything just as Poppa would. Now you've done gone and got married! Our parents would be so happy right now. You've really grown into a fine man, and they would be honored to have seen you mature."

"Awa... Shucks, sis- I couldn't have done any of it without you at my side and taking care of me. And Sadie, it really is going to all be ok, alright.

Sadie knew just what he was referring to. Her face felt warm and she was scared to speak for the emotion that would be revealed. She was still quite attached to her ranger and not ready to move on.

Kershy moved to cut in on Ollie, "I'd like to dance with the sweet lass." The music was cheerful and bubbly.

"Mr. McDougal, I need to share something with you." Sadie began.

"Call me Kershy, lass, we are family now."

"Well it's about...Be-" She didn't make it the length of the song or the end of the thought. A scraggily, toothless cowpoke cut in. He was in fact, the admirer who had been, making eyes at her all evening. He smelled-ripe, really just downright awful! He'd missed his spring bath and reeked of rotten potatoes and cow poo. Sadie was trying very hard not to be rude as she accepted. The up-swinging waltz had him turning her in deliberate nauseating circles. She was losing track of Ollie and Kershy.

A figure in the far distance caught her eye as she spun around. Was is the silhouette of a man that she knew or used to know? She feared she was hallucinating from the smell. She blinked her eyes to clear her vision. The figure leaned heavy to one side as though he compensated for a wound. She squinted at every turn in the dance to see the face of the familiar man. The darkness away from the tent was keeping his identity a mystery. She glanced back in a panic over her shoulder. The man and the horse don't match. No. It couldn't be! She chastised herself for even thinking it was possible. She was torturing herself- seeing what was not really there.

"Sadie! Get a hold of yourself." She scolded herself in her mind, averting her eyes in any direction other than the "rotten potato" cowboy standing before her. The pit of her stomach was churning and she felt dizzy with confusion. The world before her blackened as she collapsed, right there in the middle of everyone, in the arms of a stinky cow hand!

Chapter 33

"She needs some roooom." Mrs. MacDougal shouted as she came rushing and fluttering over to Sadie. "Bess dear, fetch me a cloth with some cool water."

"Yes Ma'am."

Ollie came rushing to his sister's side. "Has she eaten today, do you know?"

"I've not seen her eat a bite all the day-"the hostess replied. "Let's get her up and off the ground."

Bess returned with a cool rag and a piece of bread. Ollie started to pick her up, and there standing over them both was a man no one thought they'd ever see again!

"Ham, well glory be- where did you come from? Not waiting for an answer he continued. "It's Sadie! She's passed out from exhaustion."

"It's good to see you too- Ollie, here, let me." He reached down and scooped the limp Sadie up and began heading over to the nearest wagon. That face was just as he remembered- so sweet, smooth, and perfect.

"Now wait just one minute; that there is my woman. Who are you and where do you think you are carrying her off to?" The snaggled- toothed cowboy stood blocking Ham's path. He stood wide, puffing out his chest with a direct challenge to the ranger.

"Listen here friend, you'll be clearing a path right directly. "

"I'd do as he says, D." Ollie stated.

The cowboy stepped aside, launching a stream of tobacco from his mouth and a mumbled "It ain't over, friend."

Ham walked away with Sadie still unchanged in his arms. Bess had returned with a few pillows to prop under her head and a quilt just in case it was needed. Mrs. MacDougal busied herself making a quick pallet on the back of the wagon, and Ham gently laid her on it. Ham took the cloth and dabbed her face, cooling her warm skin and hoping she'd open those emerald eyes he longed to see. After a few minutes, the onlookers began drifting away back to the tent. The women left her in Ham's charge, as he promised that he'd call out at the first need of anything.

The two were finally alone. There was a slight cool breeze, Ham inhaled the fresh air deep in his lungs and looked toward the heavens.

"Dear God, I ask you to return this sweet precious Sadie girl to me. Heal her body, Lord, and renew her spirit. I ask this in Jesus' name- Amen.

She was still cradled in his arm and he'd not moved an inch away. He had just moved the curl from her face when she opened her eyes ever so slowly, without saying a word. A single tear rolled down her face. Unbelieving the vision before her, she dared not speak for fear he would be lost from her mind forever. "I love you Sadie girl- I've come back for you," Ham spoke in a whisper.

"Am I dreaming, Ham, or are you real?

"Yes, I am real." He reached down to wipe the tear away with his hand. It tore at him that he'd broken her heart. It was because of her that he found Jesus and his way back. He had more love and affection for her that ought to be allowed, he thought. He pulled her tight against him with a embrace that neither of them wanted to end.

"What took you so long?" Sadie said, as she stared into his brown eyes, noticing the rough stubble that was evidence he'd been riding hard in the saddle for days.

"It was a short journey out but such a long journey home." Ham leaned in for a soft sweet taste of her lips. He felt her heave a sigh of relief and melt even further in his arms.

"I'm very glad that you made the long journey home." Sadie whispered.

"Good, cause I'm never leaving you again. Now, where is that preacher man? He and I need to have us a little talk!"

●

As Sadie feeling noticeably better, Ham helped her down out of the wagon and they returned to the wedding party. Ham had made the suggestion to return to the crowd for both of their benefit, as he was feeling compelled to invite more than just a kiss. One of the men fetched over a rocking chair for Sadie to sit in and made sure she was comfortable with a glass of lemonade.

"Sadie, I've got something for you. I'll be right back, I promise." Ham let go of her hand pausing at the touch of her finger tips, and turning to take long strides out and away from the tent back into the dark evening. The gravity of the whole event was settling in. Sitting alone, Sadie felt so embarrassed for falling out that way in front of everyone. What must everyone be thinking? She smoothed her dress and imagined that she must have dirt all over her backside and face. However, her ranger was back to stay, and that's all that mattered. She couldn't help feeling blind to the world around her when he was near. The smile she'd misplaced had resumed in full force.

Bess and Meredith came to check on her, and they all noticed the group of whispering bonnets huddled over on the outskirts of the tent by the food tables. They most

184

likely were making great conversations at Sadie's expense, no doubt coming up with their own explanations.

D. the smelly ranch hand, appeared from nowhere. His demeanor was increasingly odious and he was more aggressive in his tone. With grit in his teeth and gravel in his voice, he weaved about wagging his index finger in her face. Clearly drunk and almost crossing the line of belligerence, this man had lost all of his sanity.

"I've come for ya! I aim for you to be my wife!" D slurred out the words, turning up his flask again for another drop.

"I beg your pardon, Mister. I hardly know you." Sadie responded. She instantly felt threatened and leaned forward, looking for Ollie or Ham.

"I's seent you looking my way. No matter woman, I'll fetch the preacher and you'll be going to my bunk this night."

"I will NOT!" She stood up, with a stomp of her feet and green eyes glowing.

"Don't sass me woman, go on now - get and let's go." He commenced to pulling her, as he'd taken hold of her arm. She wiggled to get free from his grip, causing quite a stir. Their struggle had chairs falling over, and everyone's attention diverted toward the scuffle. Ollie came over, hearing the loudmouth from a distance. "What's the trouble? Do we have a problem here?"

"This here woman is mine- I stake my claim."

Sadie's jaw dropped open with a look of unbelief. "This toothless cowboy must have fallen off of his horse one too many times! I am not a piece of property- unhand me!" Ollie didn't have a gun. It was his wedding day, and after all, he wasn't figuring on needing one. He advanced forward to the cowboy anyhow.

"I'll ask you, just this once, to unhand my sister!"

"Just back up, ole whitey, you ain't even wearing a gun! This is how this is going to go. I'm a-fixing get hitched to this here filly." Sadie relaxed a bit upon seeing her brother ball up his fist. Ollie made a move to grab Sadie's arm, but D. countered by whipping his pistol out with his other hand. He was wagging it around inches from Ollie's face in front of the growing crowd of friends and family.

Putting his hands up at the sight of the loaded gun, Ollie took a step back. "Let's just all calm down. My sister is feeling poorly. I don't think you know what you are talking about.- You need to head on back to the bunk house and sleep it off. Everything will look right in the morning."

D. looked Ollie squarely in the eyes and blinked to refocus, aiming the six-shooter at him straight. Ollie froze in position, not wanting to make any sudden moves to set this tipsy cowhand off. By now everyone's attention had been diverted to the fray. Once again the kids had stopped playing, the women stopped talking, and the men gathered round. Sadie stood with fright, not

wanting anyone she loved to get hurt. Kershy and
Wildcat Morrell had started in large strides across the
pasture returning to the tent. Ham was returning with
something in his hands, but she couldn't make it out. He
passed it off to a little girl with blonde hair and a tattered
apron, leaning down and whispering something to her.

D. had his back to Ham's approach. He was
slobbering drunk and very unpredictable. Ham had
always felt like it was a mite unfair to shoot a drunk man,
especially because he didn't have all his facilities. This
was no ordinary situation; there was not time to talk it out
or reason with the man. He drew his revolver and
gripped the barrel of the gun, never slowing in step or
carrying any hesitation in his movement. Simultaneously
Sadie had stepped hard on top of the cowboy's boot.
Ollie grabbed his hat and pulled it down over his eyes,
then Ham used the butt of his gun and hit him hard in the
head. D. fell to the ground, dropping his gun and loosing
Sadie's arm.

"He'll bother you no more, Sadie." Ham said as
he took her again into his arms and held her firmly
against his racing heart. He'd not shown fear, but it had
been there. "Thank You, God." Ham whispered.

Kershy and the cowhands came to collect the
unconscious cowboy and put him where he could bother
no one else that night. Sadie explained to her brother that
she would very much like to go home; she'd had more
than enough excitement for one day! Ham volunteered to
take her on his horse to leave the wagon for Ollie and
Alison.

Gathering her things, Sadie felt scatterbrained and struggled to think. She had brought dishes of food and she couldn't quite locate all of her items. Mrs. McDougal was kind and gracious to offer to sort it all out and send it with Ollie in the wagon when they returned. Seeing she could do no more, Sadie headed over to Ham and his horse. "I'm ready to go. What do you have there?"

He handed the whimpering little puppy to Sadie and immediately said, "Here hold this!" She laughed, remembering the chicken in the woods.

"What's this little fellow for?" As she held him close he was licking her face, seemingly happy to be in her arms.

"That there is your belated Christmas present. He is a blue lacey. Pretty little thing isn't' he? He'll need a name and a home- I was hoping you could help a little guy out." Ham grinned.

"You sure are right, he is adorable, and where on earth did you find him?"

"At Fort Boggy, that's a long story for on the way home. Here, let me help you into the saddle." Ham took the puppy back and dropped a hand for her to catch a boost up on the tall mare. He passed the puppy back and leapt up onto the horse, sitting behind the saddle.

"Is that where you went earlier? To get the puppy?"

"Yes, and Wildcat and Kershy cornered me for, well, it's a long story for on the way home."

Nudging the mare's flank, Ham started off. "This here horse is young, but real smart." He knew Sadie had a list of questions that would occupy his ride all the way back to the Hartmann Homestead. He had no rush at all – he'd answer every one of them twice if needed!

"Thank You God, for my Sadie girl!" Ham thought silently.

Chapter 34

It had been an enlightening ride home for them. They took turns and shared of their trials and struggles apart. Ham told Sadie of his sickness and Flip's lameness. He told of his time at Coleto Creek, his fight with God, and his final surrender to the Lord. Sadie's heart leapt with joy and love as he shared. He *was* changed! God had forgiven him and taken that old angry, silent heart to make him new.

Sadie shared with him about the letter, her hopeless days, and a concerning conversation with Manatoa. They sat on the porch with coffee, talking, till Ollie and Alison arrived in the early hours of daylight. They just didn't want the day to end and it hadn't- they stayed up all night till dawn. For all the commotion of the past day it had been a blessed one.

Sadie felt so much compassion for the little Indian boy; she believed his whole story. Ollie was still skeptical. She felt sure he was telling the truth. Why else would he risk so much for nothing to gain? As much as she didn't want to let go of Ham, she asked him to ride over to Alabama Ferry to make some inquiries. "A man with a badge and purpose tends to get a few more answers than just an ole homesteader." Sadie said playfully. If a ranger wasn't good for that then what could he do? Ham was all too happy to use his talent to find out some information for Sadie, but he hadn't made up his mind on the subject. He knew there was most likely quite a bit more to this story. He had a few other orders of business of his own he'd like to check on while at the ferry, but for the present day, they relaxed, doing only chores needed and having a much needed nap.

●

Ham rode into the ferry town the following day early, looking as if he had no particular plan. He would just see how things played out, hoping he'd return with an answer for Sadie. He'd start over at the livery and see to his horse, keeping an eye out for those Hanson boys. Ollie had filled him on their desire for mischief. He missed Flip something awful, but the bay mare wasn't bad at all. Sadie and Alison had given him a list of a few staples they needed from Hanson's General Store. He had a few other things he wanted to look for while he was there.

Alabama Ferry was a busy little town. The frequent stops of the steam boats up the river in the winter and spring kept the town bustling with action. It was a prominent staging port on the Trinity River for the area. Clean shaven, rested, and set for action, Ham dismounted and tied the mare to the hitching post. He called out, but the farrier was nowhere to be seen. No matter, he'd take a walk. He followed the trail that Ollie had described down to the burnt school house. The pile of rubbish had been cleared away and new construction had begun. Ollie had also made mention of the wandering wino that he'd paid for the slight dab of information. There was no sheriff in this town because many of the small towns couldn't afford a paid law man and left matters up to individuals. There were ladies in country dress crossing the street with places to be, and a few men were working on the school house. He made some inquiries here and there, and most folks were reluctant to share, even with his badge present and on display.

Ham stepped into Hope's Café for a bite to eat; there was a few customers, one of them was a thin lady with a large hat and stiff elbow. Her companion was a short well-dressed man, most assuredly not from Texas. A couple of other ranch hands looked like they were still trying to wake up from their hangovers with a good grump on.

"I'm Hope. What'll it be, mister?"

"I'll have the special and a coffee." She was of average height for a woman, with stringy brown hair tied back in a bun. She looked as though she had some pretty tough days in her face. She had a birthmark on her cheek that stretched to under her chin, and a serious, no-nonsense look in her eyes.

The waitress turned and walked back to the far side of the room, grabbing a cup and the hot pot off of the stove. She returned and set the cup down on the table and began to fill it. He made sure to speak discreetly as not to draw any attention from the others. "I need to find a drunk wino who tells tales about the school marm." She stood stiffly raising her left eyebrow ever so slowly, then she turned around, making no noise and walked away. "Well, there went that idea," Ham thought to himself. She returned directly with a plate of stew, which was mostly potatoes and carrots, with a little beef chipped up in it. It did smell good for what it was worth. She leaned forward and topped off his coffee cup and said, "The man you need is out behind the general store sleeping it off." He gave her a prompt wink of the eye, and she turned and headed back to fill other cups around the room.

He finished up his plate and dropped his coins on the table, tipped his hat, and with a jingle of spurs he stepped quickly with a purpose out the door. He strolled between the buildings in the alleyway pulling out his pistol and checking his shot. He didn't know what he was fixing to come up against and he wanted to be prepared. If the town was covering something up, it was his duty to figure it out. Whether or not it would be prosecuted was another matter entirely.

He found his way around the clutter to the rear of the buildings. There were empty crates, empty wash tubs, and firewood scattered about. There were rows of laundry with linens flapping in the wind. Startled by the slam of a door, he spun around to see the kitchen maid sling a pail of water out the back door. Ham took in a deep breath. Continuing his pursuit he began walking around behind the stores. Lying in a heap of broken crates and rotten hay, there was the man he was looking for! He fit the description Ollie had given him to the letter. He was out cold, smelly, foul, scruffy and drunk. Well, this will take a bit more time, Ham realized.

He fetched the mare, still standing unattended over at the livery. He lifted the motionless old wino over the saddle and quietly led him some length out of town. A mile or so down river should be far enough, he thought. He didn't want to take a chance of being accidentally interrupted by wanderers or the sound of their conversation carrying in the wind by the water. He gathered some dry wood and put the coffee on. The old feller would need a whole pot before he was any good.

The vagabond slowly began to come around. "UH oh, my head...I need a drink. Say, where am I? Who are you? Have you got a flask on you, Son?"

"My name is Ham Abner. I'm a Texas Ranger and you are going to Austin to stand trial for the murder of Elizabeth Isaacs."

"What...you've got the wrong man. Listen, I really need that drink-." Frantic, and attentive now with his wrists and ankles bound, he was rolling around in the sand trying to get upright.

"Are you Jimmy Harris? Ham began his interrogation.

"Yes. But it no matter, boy... You have the wrong man!" he snarled defensively.

"Well you see here this paper? It says I have the right to take you to Austin either way- I can. Now if you wanted to tell me a story, I might be in the listening mood."

"Is that all the coffee you have? You are going to need to put another pot! Jimmy growled. "You've been by the Hanson's General Store with your questions?"

"Yeah? What of it? Just keep going on." Ham responded.

"Awe... I shouldn't be tell 'in you this. He's going to be awful mad."

"Well, it's your trial." Ham leaned back, stretching his legs and pretending to shut his eyes.

"Can you untie me? I can't think with my hands tied."

"Mmm...well I'm going to catch me a nap before we ride out. Well, I will ride out and you will walk. I think we'll take the Old San Antonio Road." Ham tipped his hat down over his eyes and appeared to doze. The man decided to begin his story-

"Hanson has two sons close in age named Rex and Jep. They are wild boys, always up to no good. They are wild heathens, running around town always making mischief for people. They have their fun with me more than anyone. Then need a good whipping- that's what they need!

Their Ma was killed by an Indian raid when their family first came to this country. All they had was their wagon on their homestead. She hid the boys when she saw the Indians crest the hill. The boys were just little tots and she hid them under the floor in the wagon where Hanson had made a hideaway under a false floor for valuables. As I heard the tale, Hanson was out hunting some game. She tried to fend them off but was no match for them wild Indians. They killed her right in front of the young boys who were hiding. They would have burned the wagon if it hadn't been for a group of cowboys that rode up. The war party lit out of there whooping and hollering. Hanson blamed himself for leaving her alone that day. The whole clan has a healthy distaste for the red man in any variety." Jim paused.

"So what's all that have to do with the school marm?" Ham questioned.

"The boys didn't mean for anyone to get hurt. I don't reckon they did. They just wanted to scare off the Indian boy. At first he came after school for lessons once a week or so."

"What Indian boy?"

"That Indian boy that roams these parts. Well, Miss Isaacs asked him to come in during class. Not all the students or parents welcomed the idea of their kids taking lessons with an Indian. On the day of the fire, Jep and Rex refused to sit alongside an Indian in their class. One of the boys grabbed the can of coal oil during the commotion of students leaving the school for the day."

"Where'd they get the coal oil from?" Ham topped off his coffee cup, while Jimmy kept on talking.

"Awaa... Ms. Isaacs kept some available in the classroom for the lamp. Hanson carries it in his store. Most of the families in these parts have the same oil. When class dismissed Miss Isaacs asked the Indian boy to stay on for extra tutoring. The boys tossed the open can into the coals in the wood stove. The boys hid over behind the water trough at the livery and no one thought anything of it. Those boys have played all over town their whole life. I was having a drink with my best gal over on a porch nearby. Those were the good ole days. Have I told you about Mildred? She was a doll. She had the best looking legs in these parts."

"Stay focused, Jim- the boys! What did the boys do next?" Ham leaned over and untied the man's hands while he continued talking.

"Much obliged to ya," Jim continued as he rubbed his wrists. "Jep and Rex stood up to walk over toward the school house, and a boom shook the whole town! The walls and windows rattled all around. The horses ran in every direction, spooked by the noise and the sight of red flames erupting out of the school building. The fire took hold so fast! The one-room schoolhouse that doubled as a Sunday meeting house was completely engulfed in flames. It burned so hot and fast that one bucket of water was like spitting on a forest fire. The worry was that it was going to catch and burn down the rest of the town. I don't know how that boy made it out of there. We never found his body."

"Why have you never reported this?"

"Reported it? To who exactly? Hanson runs this town, in case you missed it and he's a real unhappy feller and has the only general store for miles around. He promised to keep me in a supply of drink if I told tales of how that Indian boy was to blame. You still gonna take me in?" Ham reached over and topped off his cup.

"I outa but, Nah, you're not worth the trip to Austin," Ham tossed the blank paper into the fire.

"Can you find your way back to town?"

"Yeah."

"Good, cause I never saw you."

Chapter 35

Ham returned to the Homestead and shared all that he'd learned. Sadie's heart was broken for the lad. Ollie was beginning to be won over, but he was still being skeptical, even after breaking bread with the boy. Alison attended the kitchen, making preparations for the evening meal.

"Sadie, would you go for a walk with me?" Ham asked quietly. Sadie glanced over at Alison to see if she were feeling competent in handling the meal. She smiled widely and motioned with the hot cloth as though she were shooing her out of the house. "Sure, that would be lovely," she answered.

"Ollie, Alison, we aren't going far," Ham declared as they walked out of the cabin and started across the property. Passing the corral Sadie realized they were going toward her favorite spot on the property, the cliffing hill. Sadie was rattling on about the new chickens, grapes for jelly and juice, and all their plans for the summer. She was so pretty when she talked about anything, Ham thought. Those smile lines and green eyes made his heart melt.

"Sadie, I need to say something."

"Well, go ahead. Isn't this view beautiful? All of the trees have bloomed," she chatted nervously.

"Yes, but, Sadie-"

She had a flutter in her stomach. She had the sensation that Ham was going to say something really important. She looked at him and fought the nervous urge to babble, pausing for him to speak.

"Sadie girl, I don't have a cabin, chickens or even a homestead. I have a lame horse over close to the Navasota that probably thinks I've abandoned him. I have a job and a post. I'll be gone a lot and the job is dangerous, but I can't see living life without you any longer. If you are willing I'll give you all that I have. If you'd consider my offer...........well, I'd be honored if you'd marry me."

"Yes."

"Yes you'll consider it?"

"No silly, ---- Yes, I'll marry YOU!"

She jumped up into his arms and he spun her around. There was a squeal in her voice and the delight in both their faces. Anyone would know that they both had made their long journey home and found each other there.

"Now, how about that riding lesson?"

From the Author

I am so glad that you chose to spend some time in just one year of the life of the Hartmann family on their homestead. Many people during this time had such life-changing hardships and had to learn to lean on God for their strength. No doubt the adventure in deep East Texas is not over for Ollie and Alison nor for Ham and Sadie. I hope you've seen a glimpse of God's grace and goodness through their eyes and have seen how simple it is to lean upon His everlasting arms in your daily life.

Blessings,

Celina

Made in the USA
Columbia, SC
13 September 2018